u
."

"Yeah, I [...] clueless not to k[...]

"Well, what do you think? Have they convinced you?"

And what about you? The phrase flitted through Brittany's mind. Thankfully, she hadn't voiced the thought aloud. Brittany held a smile in place, hoping that her thoughts weren't transparent as she found herself wishing Parker showed as much enthusiasm about her taking the job as the girls did.

"Does your silence mean you're going to turn us down?"

"It means I haven't made up my mind." Brittany continued to stare out the window. She didn't want to look at him for fear that he could tell how his nearness made her insides a jumble. If the choice was only about Rose and Jasmine, the decision would be easy. But the fact that her boss would be a handsome man who made her heart trip gave her pause.

Books by Merrillee Whren

Love Inspired

The Heart's Homecoming
An Unexpected Blessing
Love Walked In
The Heart's Forgiveness
Four Little Blessings
Mommy's Hometown Hero
Homecoming Blessings
*Hometown Promise
*Hometown Proposal
*Hometown Dad
Montana Match

*Kellerville

MERRILLEE WHREN

is the winner of the 2003 Golden Heart Award, presented by Romance Writers of America, for best inspirational romance manuscript. In 2004, she made her first sale to Steeple Hill Books. She is married to her own personal hero, her husband of thirty-plus years, and has two grown daughters. She has lived in Atlanta, Boston, Dallas and Chicago but now makes her home on one of God's most beautiful creations, an island off the east coast of Florida. When she's not writing or working for her husband's recruiting firm, she spends her free time playing tennis or walking the beach, where she does the plotting for her novels. Please visit her website, www.merrilleewhren.com.

Montana Match

Merrillee Whren

Love Inspired

Recycling programs
for this product may
not exist in your area.

™ LOVE INSPIRED BOOKS

ISBN-13: 978-0-373-87719-5

MONTANA MATCH

www.LoveInspiredBooks.com

Printed in U.S.A.

Dear Reader,

Welcome to Love Inspired!

2012 is a very special year for us. It marks the fifteenth anniversary of Love Inspired. Hard to believe that fifteen years ago, we first began publishing our warm and wonderful inspirational romances.

Back in 1997, we offered readers three books a month. Since then we've expanded quite a bit! In addition to the heartwarming contemporary romances of Love Inspired, we have the exciting romantic suspenses of Love Inspired Suspense, and the adventurous historical romances of Love Inspired Historical. Whatever your reading preference, we've got fourteen books a month for you to choose from now!

Throughout the year we'll be celebrating in several different ways. Look for books by bestselling authors who've been writing for us since the beginning, stories by brand-new authors you won't want to miss, special miniseries in all three lines, reissues of top authors and much, much more.

This is our way of thanking you for reading Love Inspired books. We know our uplifting stories of hope, faith and love touch your hearts as much as they touch ours.

Join us in celebrating fifteen amazing years of inspirational romance!

Blessings,

Melissa Endlich and Tina James
Senior Editors of Love Inspired Books

I would like to dedicate this book to the memory of my mother Gladys Luft. She instilled in me the love of a good story when she read to me at bedtime.

I would like to thank Barbara Lea Campbell for giving Bogey his name.

* * *

Do not judge, and you will not be judged.
Do not condemn, and you will not be condemned.
Forgive, and you will be forgiven. Give, and it will
be given to you. A good measure, pressed down,
shaken together and running over, will be poured
into your lap. For with the measure you use,
it will be measured to you.
—*Luke* 6:37–38

Chapter One

Thud. Thud. Thud. Books hit the floor all over the fifth-grade classroom, shattering the relative quiet. Brittany Gorman gathered her survival instincts and forced herself not to react. She tightened her grip on the chalk and continued to write the math homework assignment on the chalkboard. This bratty group of kids pulled some kind of stunt every time she substituted for their regular teacher. Today Brittany was determined not to let their misbehavior bother her.

Brittany wrote as slowly as she could. She didn't want to turn around and see the feigned innocence on their faces until she was sure she could face them with a stoic mask in place. There was no doubt that the instigator of this little trick was the class clown who called her "Miss Carrot Top" or "Miss Freckle Face" under his breath, just loud enough that she couldn't miss hearing his remarks. She always pretended not to notice.

Finally, she set the chalk in the tray and glanced at the clock before turning to the group. Some of the students had already retrieved their books, but other books still lay on the floor. She looked at the students, making eye contact with as many of them as she could before speaking. "You have twenty minutes to work on the assignment. If you have any problems, raise your hand, and I'll be glad to help you."

A few snickers drifted through the air, but Brittany chose to ignore those, too. Without making mention of the book incident, she roamed up and down the aisles between the desks. She breathed a sigh of relief as further conflict faded. Despite situations like this, substitute teaching was still the best of all the bad temp jobs she had tried since she'd lost her position as a financial planner. Glancing out the window at the snowy Montana landscape, she prayed that all would go well until the final bell. While she waited for that sound of freedom, she vowed to double her efforts to find a real job—one that didn't involve kids.

Half an hour later, Brittany fled out a side door and searched the school's parking lot for her ride. She spotted her roommate's sporty silver compact car and dashed toward it. She opened the door and hopped in.

Glancing at Brittany, Heather Watson maneuvered her way to the main road, her dark eyes full of curiosity. "You seem to be in a hurry to get away."

Brittany leaned back on the headrest. "What a day! It didn't end soon enough."

"Want to tell me about it?"

"No. I don't want to relive it. I can sum it up in one word. Dreadful."

"That bad?"

"Worse. I'm beginning to think I'm just not good with kids."

"Not true. The kids in the church youth group love you."

"Thanks for your vote of confidence." Brittany smiled halfheartedly. "I guess it's just that one horrible class of fifth graders that drives me crazy."

Heather nodded. "Is your car ready?"

"Yes, but I'm afraid to see the repair bill." Brittany released a harsh breath. "That car is falling to pieces one part at a time. It's a money pit, but without a regular job, there's no way I can buy a new one."

"Well, at least they could fix it."

"I guess I should look on the bright side." Brittany forced a smile. "It's a good thing that today is your day off. Thanks for picking me up."

"No problem." Heather turned onto the street where the car dealership was located. "Are you subbing tomorrow?"

"Not yet, but I could get a call early in the morning. After today, I'm not sure I could bring myself to say yes."

"Then don't. Come skiing with me."

"You know I can't afford to go skiing, especially now with the added expense for my car."

Brittany wished Heather could understand the stress of not having a real job. The need to find steady employment constantly weighed on her mind. And now that she'd broken up with Max, the one reason for staying in Billings no longer existed. She needed to widen her job search.

"I told you that won't be a problem. My uncle Parker pays for everything, even guests. He does this every year for our family on the Martin Luther King holiday weekend."

"I thought I'd met all your dad's siblings. How come I've never met your uncle?"

"Because he's a reclusive bachelor who lives on a ranch about fifty miles from Billings. I call him my mad scientist uncle because he's always working on some kind of invention. We only see him on this ski trip and maybe out at his place on the Fourth of July. And at Christmas. Otherwise, he keeps pretty much to himself on that ranch."

Brittany thought the guy sounded pretty weird, but she didn't want to say anything bad about him. "I'd hate to impose."

Heather gave Brittany a challenging look. "You won't

impose. You need a change of scenery, so you can forget about the loss of your job and the breakup with your worth- less boyfriend."

Brittany shook her head. "Going on a ski vacation isn't going to help me find a job or make me forget Max."

"Max is very forgettable. You shouldn't waste time think- ing about him. You never know. Maybe you'll meet someone who's looking to hire a good financial planner or accountant."

"You are such an optimist."

Brittany was beginning to question her decision to stay in Billings after she'd lost her job, but she had wanted to remain there because of her relationship with Max.

More than ever, she wanted to prove to her parents that she could make the right choices. She had to show them that they hadn't wasted their money on her college degree. That meant widening her search for a good financial job. From the be- ginning, they'd wanted her to forge her own path rather than follow Max to Montana. Would going home to the Spokane area mean she'd have to admit they'd been right? Could she make the right decision this time?

Giggles floated through the air as Parker Watson entered the kitchen of the six-bedroom, cedar-sided house he'd rented for the annual family ski trip. He relished the sound of har- mony coming from Rose and Jasmine, his six-year-old twin daughters, who were having breakfast at the table in the eating area off the kitchen. He stared at the cup of coffee sitting on the counter and wished that somehow a nanny for his girls would appear out of the steam rising from it—like a genie from a bottle.

He was working on a big project that could lead to more medical writing jobs. He was already behind schedule be- cause he'd had to take over the homeschooling duties that had been Jenny's domain. If he was going to give full attention to his work, he had to find a good caregiver now.

He picked up the cup and moseyed over to the table. "Are you girls finished with breakfast? The ski slopes are waiting for us."

Rose took the last gulp of milk, then nodded her head, her dark braids swinging across her shoulders. "I'm done."

"Me, too." Jasmine jumped up from her chair.

As Rose joined her sister, Parker patted each of them on the head. "Then you need to put on your ski clothes."

"We will." Their voices echoed around the vaulted ceiling as they raced for the stairs.

Parker cupped his hands around his mouth. "Don't forget to brush your teeth."

The girls stopped and leaned over the balustrade that surrounded the loft at the top of the stairs. "We won't."

"Sounds like they're pretty excited about today." Delia chuckled.

Parker turned to his housekeeper. "I hope they get along. All I've done the past couple of weeks is break up fights."

"You know it started right after Jenny, Mark and their kids moved away. The girls lost an important person in their lives, and it's upset their whole routine."

"I know, but that doesn't mean they should misbehave." Parker sighed. "I wish Mark hadn't taken that job in Colorado, but I can't blame him for taking a better opportunity. It's tough losing a foreman and the girls' teacher and caregiver all at once. Since I started advertising for a nanny, I've had exactly one inquiry. And as soon as the woman found out that the position was on an isolated Montana ranch, she wasn't interested."

"You know what I've said about that." Delia gave him a no-nonsense look—the kind she always gave him when she was trying to make a point. "Folks who live closer to the ranch won't have a problem with the location."

"I don't know why you think I'll find a nanny in Stockton. The people in that town have no use for me, and I have no use for them."

Delia's wrinkled face brightened, and she winked. "Heather might know someone. Maybe that friend she's bringing with her?"

"You are such an optimist." Parker rubbed the back of his neck and gave Delia a wry smile before turning his attention to the noisy footsteps on the stairs. "Sounds like the girls are ready. Tell Heather and her friend to head up to the slopes when they get here."

Hours later, Parker stepped into the ski lodge and, as he'd promised Heather minutes before, searched the room for a petite redhead. The color of her hair should make her easy to find. He wasn't looking forward to meeting Heather's friend, but he was doing this to please his favorite niece.

The smell of burgers and fries wafted his way as he walked farther into the Main Lodge restaurant. Finally, he spotted an attractive young woman with bright coppery hair that fell around her shoulders. She sat alone at a table near the wall of windows looking out at the mountain.

Her expression told him she was deep in thought about something that didn't make her happy. He could relate to that look.

He stepped forward. "Excuse me. Are you Brittany Gorman?"

She stared up at him, her appearance still somber. Her light brownish-green eyes held a puzzled look. "Yes. How do you know my name?"

"I'm Parker Watson, Heather's uncle."

"You're Heather's uncle?" The pitch of her voice rose along with her eyebrows.

"I am. Is there a problem?" Parker tried not to frown.

Could she possibly know about his past—seen him on the news when he'd been falsely accused of an inappropriate relationship with one of his high-school students? According to Heather, Brittany had moved to Billings about six years ago, after the scandal had subsided, but that was no guarantee. He knew firsthand how malicious gossip could linger.

Despite being innocent, he'd never gotten his life back. In the beginning, he'd tried to repair his reputation, but the hushed conversations and whispered innuendos had followed him. Frustrated and hurt over the way his former friends and colleagues had turned against him, he'd decided things would be easier if he gave up teaching and kept to himself on the ranch.

She grimaced, a blush creeping up her freckled face. "I'm sorry. I didn't mean to be so abrupt. It's just that…well, I expected you to be older…much older."

"So that's why you seemed startled?"

Nodding, she placed a hand over her heart. "When Heather was talking about her uncle, I had this picture in my mind of a man about the age of her father with a salt-and-pepper beard."

Realizing that she didn't know anything about his past, Parker let his relief come bubbling out in a chuckle. "I'm twenty-five years younger than Heather's dad and only seven years older than Heather. She seems more like a cousin than a niece. I figured out a long time ago that I was my parents' 'oops' baby."

"Oh." She looked away, as if his statement had embarrassed her.

He'd probably given her more information than she wanted to know. He had a bad habit of speaking his mind, no matter what the consequences. Better change the subject. "Heather told me you took a ski lesson this morning?"

"Yeah. Where is Heather?"

"Still on the slopes, but she sent me down here to check on you. How did the lesson go?"

Brittany shrugged. "Okay, I guess. I learned how to snow-plow."

"That's a good start. Are you ready for lunch?"

Brittany nodded. "I thought Heather was meeting me."

"She is, but she wanted to do a little skiing with Rose and Jasmine first before the girls did their afternoon thing."

He was out of practice talking with single women who were close to his own age. What did it matter? He wasn't going to see Brittany again after this weekend. Even if she was pretty, he didn't need to impress her. "Do you mind if I join you while we wait for Heather?"

She looked up at him in surprise. "I'm sorry. I should've invited you to sit with me. I don't know where my manners have gone. Please, join me. In fact, I'm glad to have a chance to talk to you. I want to thank you. It's really generous of you to pay for everything, especially since I'm not family."

"Think nothing of it." Parker smiled. He pulled out a chair and sat across from her.

Now what did he say? He hated small talk, especially since he seldom had face-to-face interaction with anyone except the people on the ranch and an occasional family member. It was better for him and the twins to be surrounded by people who supported and accepted them. But in his efforts to shield his girls from malicious gossip, he'd gotten out of practice at making conversation with strangers.

Parker tried to lasso his thoughts, but her cute freckled face had his mind in a dither. Maybe that's why she had him noticing things about her that he shouldn't be noticing at all.

"Heather tells me you live on a ranch."

"Yeah." An invitation to talk about himself—one of his least favorite things to do. When he was with his family, all he wanted to talk about was his girls, but he didn't want to explain to a stranger why he was a bachelor father.

"Do you raise cattle?"

"I'm more of a gentleman rancher."

"A what?"

"I don't actually do any ranching. I only live there."

"Oh." The word was wrapped in curiosity.

Hoping to avoid giving her any other information, he ignored her questioning look. "What about you? What do you do?"

Brittany stared at him for a moment, then glanced away toward the windows. Sighing heavily, she looked back at him. "I'm currently a substitute teacher. I lost my *real* job a few months ago. I tried some temp jobs, but they were short-lived. Then a teacher I know from church suggested that I sign up to be a substitute, but that still makes for a rather unsettled life—not knowing how much will be in my next paycheck. It's hard to find regular work of any kind."

Parker couldn't help remembering Delia's speculation about Brittany being a prospect for the nanny position. His desperation to find someone to care for his daughters was making him have irrational thoughts. He knew very little about this young woman. "What was your previous job?"

"I worked for a financial-planning company, and they were downsizing. I was the last hired and the first fired." Brittany laughed halfheartedly.

"Any job prospects in your field?" Now Parker knew what had caused her troubled look. He'd like to commiserate, but he certainly didn't want to explain the false accusations that had cost him his job. The unfairness of it all still troubled him.

She shook her head. "I'm just trying to figure out what

I'm going to do next. Kind of puts a damper on trying to have fun."

"Maybe we can get you up on the slopes and take your mind off it for at least a little while." And his mind, too.

"Heather said the same thing." Brittany smiled.

"Then we'll try not to mention it again." Taking in that smile, Parker tried to ignore the way his heart bumped against his ribs. Another reason not to entertain the idea of her as a nanny. Having a nanny he was attracted to would be a big mistake.

"I'm not sure that will help. I keep thinking about it. Can I find a new job in Billings, or should I go back home? If I choose to go home, how will that affect Heather, since I share an apartment with her?"

Parker took in the fact that Brittany, despite her own troubles, was still concerned about Heather. Brittany's thoughtfulness said something very good about her. "So where's home?"

"Pinecrest, a little town north of Spokane, Washington."

Glancing toward the door and hoping to see Heather, Parker nodded. "Yeah. I know Spokane. I've been there several times."

"But I'll bet you've never been to Pinecrest."

"You'd be correct."

"Not many job prospects there, but maybe I can find one in Spokane." Brittany sighed. "I think my parents want me to move back. My dad's checking out jobs in Spokane for me. He says the sooner I get back into finance the better. Temp jobs and substitute teaching don't exactly enhance my resume."

"What brought you to Montana in the first place?"

Brittany sighed. "My boyfriend Max. He came to college here on a football scholarship."

A boyfriend. That bit of information ought to keep his wayward thoughts in check. "So what does he do?"

"He's in graduate school, but, actually, he's not my boyfriend anymore. We just broke up last weekend. So that's why I'm thinking about moving back to Washington." Brittany's green eyes shimmered, and she looked away toward the window. "That's another reason Heather invited me to ski. She thought it might help me forget the breakup."

No boyfriend after all. He knew the hurt of a broken relationship—what it meant to have people you trusted turn away when you needed them the most. Did he detect unshed tears? He was surprised to find himself wanting to comfort her. The urge to reach out to strangers, to help people in need, had been very rare in recent years—but Brittany seemed to bring it out in him.

"Are you okay?"

Parker's question made Brittany flush. How could she admit to this virtual stranger that part of her was glad that she and Max had finally faced the truth? She hated admitting that the breakup was inevitable, but she'd finally come to the conclusion that the relationship was at a dead end. "Yes. It was for the best."

As Brittany said the words, she was even more certain that her statement was true. But she couldn't forget that Max had been a part of her life for eight years, and his absence left an empty place in her heart.

"So, I suppose there's nothing keeping you in Billings anymore."

Before Brittany could respond, Heather approached the table as she waved a hand above her head. "I see you two found each other."

Parker stood and pulled out a chair for her. "Yeah, we were getting to know each other."

"Thanks." Heather gave her uncle a pointed look. "I'll bet you were asking all the questions, weren't you?"

"Did Rose and Jasmine get to their afternoon activity?" Parker ignored Heather's inquiry.

"They did. They settled in nicely. No problem."

"Good. I hope they enjoy themselves this afternoon as much as we did this morning. Pretty soon they're going to be skiing better than me."

Leaning back, Brittany took in the exchange. Heather was right. Parker had asked most of the questions, and he certainly looked relieved when Heather had walked in. Brittany figured that Parker wasn't exactly excited about entertaining his niece's friend. But the fact that he'd made the effort told Brittany that he was a considerate man.

After talking with Parker, Brittany concluded that he hardly seemed like the recluse Heather had described. After all, he'd apparently been skiing with Rose and Jasmine while Brittany took her ski lesson. She wondered about the two females that she hadn't met but didn't dare ask about for fear of seeming nosy. She was already worried that she'd seemed impolite by waiting so long to invite him to join her.

She'd forced herself to look out the window in order to keep from staring at him or the intensity in his coffee-colored eyes.

His handsome face, covered with dark stubble, gave him a rugged appearance. His tobacco-brown hair, in need of a trim, only added to the persona. His good looks probably went a long way in explaining the presence of Rose and Jasmine.

"So what do you think? Are you ready to try your hand at skiing after lunch?"

Brittany suddenly realized that Heather's question was aimed at her. She needed to quit thinking about Parker and pay attention to the conversation. She shrugged. "I don't know. One lesson hardly seems like enough."

"Sure it is. Besides, Parker will take you out and give you some instructions, won't you, Parker?" Heather glanced at her uncle with a sly smile.

Brittany tried to get her friend's attention, so she could signal her disapproval. "Your uncle doesn't want to be stuck skiing with me."

Heather laid a hand on Brittany's shoulder. "He doesn't mind."

Parker cleared his throat. "Ah...you're talking about me as if I'm not here. I can speak for myself."

"Okay, but you can't deny that you're a great ski instructor."

"I won't."

Heather grinned at Parker. "Then it's settled. You'd be happy to help Brittany this afternoon."

Brittany had no idea how to respond. Parker didn't look exactly thrilled, but he also seemed too polite to go against Heather's wishes. He was the ever-accommodating host.

Brittany didn't want to seem ungrateful, but she didn't want him to feel obligated to spend time with her, either. "I'd hate for you to be tied down with a beginner like me when you could be out skiing with Rose, Jasmine and Heather."

"Rose and Jasmine are occupied for the afternoon, and I'm going to do a little snowboarding. So Uncle Parker is all yours." Heather grinned again, making no attempt to disguise her triumph. "And when the slopes close, I'll meet you two at the lodge."

"That works for me," Parker said.

Manufacturing a smile, Brittany knew she was trapped. "Okay, if that's the way you guys want it."

"Good. Then it's settled." Heather stood, shrugged out of

her ski jacket and hung it over the back of the chair. "Now, let's get something to eat."

Soon they were eating a hearty lunch. At least Parker and Heather were. Brittany barely nibbled on her hamburger and fries. Her appetite had fled as her mind buzzed with thoughts of Parker, skiing and her dicey job situation. All of them gave her something to be nervous about.

Chapter Two

Thirty minutes later, Brittany held her ski poles with a death grip. She felt as though she was headed for some other world in her helmet and goggles. Her stomach churned as she followed Parker to the chairlift. Thankfully, she'd left most of her lunch on the plate. The thought of skiing down a real hill, not the bunny hill where she'd practiced earlier, terrified her.

"Why so grim? You look like you're headed to the electric chair." Chuckling, Parker stopped next to the chairlift.

She squared her shoulders and looked up at him. Should she let him know how scared she was, or should she tough it out? Who was she kidding? He probably already knew she was quaking in her ski boots. "I've never been on a lift before."

"You'll do fine. There's nothing to it. You hop on and hop off."

"Easy for you to say. You can probably do it with your eyes closed."

"Not quite." He chuckled again. "Remember. I'm here to help you."

Somehow that didn't seem reassuring at all. The whole scenario intimidated her. "So what do I do?"

"Just follow my lead. You step out here and wait for the chair to come to you." He moved closer to the lift.

"Okay." Brittany followed, holding her breath until she was seated beside Parker in the chair.

"Now that wasn't so hard, was it?"

She let her breath out in a big whoosh when they swung out over the snow-covered hillside, awash in sunshine and glistening snow. Pressing herself back against the chair, she hoped she wouldn't fall out. She didn't think she had a fear of heights, but she was beginning to wonder about that as they dangled on a cable far above the ground. She tried not to look down.

"When we get to the top, put the tips of your skis down and push out of the chair." Parker's voice cut through the fear clouding her mind for a moment, but anxiety quickly returned.

"Okay." Her pulse pounded in her head.

"Ready. Here we go."

Brittany tried to put her skis on the ground. In the next instant, she sprawled face-first in the snow as the lift ground to a halt.

"Are you all right?" Parker rushed to her side.

Mortified, she scrambled to her feet with the help of Parker and several bystanders. When she was standing upright, she wished she had somewhere to hide. Did she dare look at him? He was probably wishing Heather hadn't suggested he spend the afternoon giving ski instructions, especially with a klutz for a student. Finally, Brittany drummed up enough courage to glance up. A little smile played at the edges of Parker's mouth. She supposed he was trying not to laugh.

"I'm okay." Brushing snow off herself, Brittany wished everyone would quit fussing over her. She hated being the center of attention, especially this kind of attention. "Let's go."

"If you're sure everything's okay."

"It is."

"Good. Follow me." Parker slowly skied ahead of her to the beginning of a trail.

Brittany followed and tried to remember what she'd learned in her lesson. "Are you going first?"

"No. You go, and I'll ski behind and watch." Parker stopped at the top of the trail and glanced her way as he pulled his goggles into place.

Oh, great. He was going to watch her. Just what she didn't need. She couldn't see his eyes behind the goggles, but she feared they were probably still full of laughter. Letting out a harsh breath, she put on her goggles.

"Okay. Here I go." Her voice sounded strained even to her own ears. She pushed off with her ski poles and glided across the packed snow. She skied from side to side on the trail so she wouldn't pick up too much speed.

"Hey, you're doing great!" Parker's voice sounded over the *shush, shush, shush* sound the skis made on the snow.

Brittany tried to ignore the way his praise made her pulse quicken. She tried to convince herself that her reaction had nothing to do with the fact that he was a handsome man. After all, her experience with Max had taught her that planning her life around a man had been a mistake. His inattention had broken her heart. She'd had it with men. So why did her first encounter with another handsome man have her feeling this way?

She shook away the question and focused her mind on her technique. If she wasn't careful, she'd wind up face-first in the snow again. She had to give her full attention to skiing and forget about men.

When she reached the bottom of the trail, a true sense of accomplishment brightened her thoughts. Parker joined her and smiled. His smile took her breath away. Or was it the sudden gust of wind?

"Hey, that was a good job. Ready to go again?"

"Sure." The triumph of her first downhill trip had made her forget the embarrassment at the ski lift. Now another ride loomed before her. She wasn't going to let a ski lift intimidate her, and she certainly wasn't going to let Parker sense any of her fear. Straightening her shoulders, she headed back to the ski lift, determined to get in and out of the chair without falling.

"Hey, wait up." Parker skied up beside her. "You've taken to skiing very well."

Brittany basked in his praise, then wondered why. She shouldn't need his approval. Moving closer to the lift, she tried not to think about it. "That was fun."

"Ready for another ride on the lift?"

Brittany joined Parker in the line that waited to take the lift to the top of the ski run. "Yeah, I think I'll get it right this time."

While they waited, Parker made very little attempt at conversation. She worried that he was bored silly being with her and skiing on these easy slopes when he could readily conquer the difficult runs. She wanted to tell him that he didn't need to hang around with her, but she feared he would take it the wrong way.

So she spent the rest of the afternoon skiing on the easiest trails, either following Parker's lead as he showed her something or having him follow as he watched her. Occasionally, he gave her a simple tip or complimented her on her progress. She had to admit that he managed to keep a perfect balance between instruction and praise. Heather was right. He *was* a good teacher.

At the end of one of their runs, Parker stopped her as she headed for the lift. "You're going to wear yourself out. Don't be surprised if every muscle in your body is sore tomorrow."

"Really?"

Smiling, he nodded. "You'll discover muscles you didn't know you had."

"That doesn't sound very encouraging."

"Just letting you know what to expect." He glanced toward the lift. "It's almost four o'clock. They close the trails on the mountain at four, so we ought to head back to the lodge."

"Sure." Despite her worries, Brittany had enjoyed herself.

When they reached the lodge, Brittany began removing her skis and boots, all the while keeping an eye out for Heather. As Brittany unbuckled her boots, her cell phone buzzed, indicating a text message. She pulled it out and glanced at it. Max. She'd completely forgotten about him. Heather's plan was working.

Max wanted to know where she was. Too bad he hadn't been that concerned these past couple of years while they'd been dating. He'd been too engrossed in his studies to bother with her. Now he didn't seem to get the message that their relationship was over. Maybe he'd finally figure it out if she didn't respond. Frowning, she shoved the phone into her pocket.

When she glanced up, Parker was staring at her. "Problems?"

Brittany sighed, wishing Parker hadn't noticed. "Yeah. Someone I didn't want to talk to."

Parker's brown eyes studied her face. "That old boyfriend?"

Brittany nodded and lowered her gaze, hoping to avoid any other questions about Max.

"I didn't mean to pry. It's none of my business, but I couldn't help noticing your frown."

"That's okay." Brittany shrugged. "Thanks so much for spending your afternoon with me. I appreciate your help."

Parker gave her a wry grin. "You're welcome. I enjoyed

our afternoon together. You have the makings of a good skier."

"Thanks, but I don't plan to take up skiing, especially since I don't have a regular job." Brittany wondered whether Parker was just being polite, or whether he'd really enjoyed her company. What difference did it make? After this weekend, she'd probably never see him again. For some reason that thought made her sad.

"You can head to the lodge to meet Heather, while I pick up Rose and Jasmine." Parker gathered his boots and skis. "Tell Heather that you guys can go ahead to the house. I'll see you there."

"Okay, thanks again." Brittany made her way to the lodge while she contemplated meeting the mysterious female duo.

When Brittany arrived, Heather was already waiting. She hopped up from her chair. "Did you and Parker have a good time?"

Brittany shrugged. "We survived."

"What's that mean?"

"It means that I managed to stay upright most of the afternoon, and Parker tolerated boredom while skiing on the easy trails."

"I'm sure he had a good time. He loves to teach." Heather gave Brittany a cheesy grin.

"You're right. He was very patient with a bumbling beginner." Brittany tried to ignore Heather's speculative grin. "He told me we should go ahead to the house while he picks up Rose and Jasmine."

"Okay." Heather opened the door and headed toward the parking lot. "You're going to adore them."

As Brittany followed, she decided the time had come to ask Heather about them. "You keep talking about them, but you've never told me who they are."

Stopping, Heather looked at Brittany. "I haven't?"

"No."

"I'm sorry." Heather shook her head. "I don't know why I thought you knew. They're Parker's six-year-old twin daughters. To tell you the truth, those little girls are all that keeps him from completely turning his back on the outside world."

As Brittany walked across the parking lot, her mind spun with the information. His daughters? How totally wrong her thoughts had been. "But you said he's a bachelor."

"He is. He adopted the girls when they were babies after their mother died." Heather pulled her keys from her pocket. "She was killed by her stepfather while trying to protect her mother."

"Oh, how terrible." Brittany placed a hand over her heart. She didn't know what else to say, though her mind was full of questions. Did Parker have some connection to the deceased woman? Why didn't her family take the children? Why would a bachelor adopt two little girls? But surely it would be rude to ask.

Finally gathering her thoughts, Brittany looked at Heather over the top of the car. "Your uncle certainly has a compassionate heart."

"Yeah, he does, and it's caused him nothing but trouble."

After that, Brittany couldn't contain her curiosity. "What kind of trouble?"

"It's a long story. And a sad one." Heather opened the door to her car.

Brittany slid into the passenger seat.

The hum of the motor filled the silence while Heather drove toward the main road. She glanced at Brittany, who waited as patiently as she could for her friend to collect her thoughts. "I think you should know the story. Then you'll understand why Parker has become a recluse."

"Are you sure he wants you talking about him? After all,

it's his life, and I'm a stranger. You don't have to make explanations to me."

Heather shrugged. "But I want you to understand Parker and like him."

Brittany knit her eyebrows. "You aren't trying to push the two of us together, are you?"

Heather chuckled. "That would be rather presumptuous of me, wouldn't it?"

"Yeah, it would." Brittany took in the little smile that curved Heather's mouth. Her expression didn't ease Brittany's suspicions. "So what were you going to tell me?"

"Sydney, Rose and Jasmine's mother, was one of Parker's students."

"He's a teacher?"

"He *was* a teacher, but he's not now because of what happened." Heather was quiet for a few seconds, then glanced Brittany's way. "Parker was a very dedicated teacher. He spent lots of extra time helping students. Sydney was one of those kids. He was helping her study for her college-entrance exams, so they spent a lot of time together after school."

"Was that a problem?"

"Not until Sydney turned up pregnant. Once her pregnancy was evident, someone started a rumor that Parker was the father. It spread through the school like a cattle stampede and wound up in the ears of the school board and the superintendent. Despite Parker's and Sydney's adamant denials, he was suspended from his teaching job. The woman he was dating ended their relationship. People in the community condemned him—even people from his church."

"How terrible for him! Why didn't people believe him?" Brittany frowned.

"Good question, especially after the girls were born and paternity tests proved that Parker wasn't the father." Heather shook her head. "After that, he moved out to the ranch, and he's never been the same."

"What did your family think?"

"We never doubted Parker. Not for a minute. We couldn't believe he was being accused of such a thing." Heather shook her head. "It was really hard on Grandma and Grandpa Watson. They were in the process of moving to Arizona and almost decided not to go, but Parker insisted that they not change their plans. He always thought about others and not himself. Because he was that kind of person, no one in the family could fathom the reaction of the community."

"Me, either, and I barely know him."

"I'm glad you feel that way." Heather smiled.

After listening to Heather's explanation, Brittany tried to process the information about Parker and reconcile it with the man she'd gotten to know this afternoon. No wonder he'd seemed so distant at first, so reluctant to talk about himself. Later on the ski slopes, he'd seemed more comfortable. Had he started to trust her not to judge him?

A few minutes later, Heather parked her car in front of a huge, two-story house, surrounded by snowy pastureland and hillsides covered with Ponderosa pine. Brittany followed Heather up the walk with snow piled high on either side. As she stepped onto the covered front porch, she took in the view. "The Beartooth Mountains are spectacular."

"You're right, and so is the house. Wait till you see the inside. Parker rents this place every year. His housekeeper, Delia, will be here, so the house should be unlocked." As Heather opened the door, a short, rotund woman with graying dark brown hair greeted them. Heather set her suitcase down and hugged the woman. "Delia, it's so good to see you. I want you to meet my friend, Brittany Gorman."

After the introductions, Brittany surveyed the spacious living room filled with leather sofas and chairs, a rustic coffee table and end tables. A Native American rug covered the plank flooring. The waning light streamed through a bank of windows on one wall that looked out on a deck and a nearby creek cutting a path through the snow-covered acreage.

"You're the first guests to arrive. Your parents called and said they'd be here by supper." Delia moseyed toward the open stairway that led to the second floor. "I'll show you your room."

"Good." Heather picked up her bag and followed Delia. "We'll have a chance to clean up before supper."

Hauling her suitcase, Brittany tagged along and marveled at the vaulted ceiling and loft overlooking the first floor. This place must have cost a mint to secure for the long holiday weekend. More questions popped into Brittany's mind. He lived on a ranch where he didn't do any ranching. So what did Parker do that allowed him to rent this enormous house and pay for a large group of his relatives to go skiing? She'd discovered a few more pieces that needed to find their places in the puzzle making up Parker Watson.

After Brittany showered and put on a pair of tan corduroys and a green wool sweater, she looked at Heather, who was still blow-drying her hair. "Is it okay if I wander around the house?"

"Sure. I'll be done in a minute and join you."

Brittany strolled into the loft area overlooking the front room and leaned her forearms on the railing. Gazing out at the magnificent view of the snow-covered mountains, she wished life didn't have to be so complicated.

As Brittany continued to take in the fabulous view, she couldn't help thinking of the scripture she'd memorized as a child. She whispered it softly to herself. "I lift up my eyes to the hills—where does my help come from? My help comes from the Lord, the Maker of heaven and earth." Did God have the answers?

Lately, she'd let her spiritual life slide. Was God trying to get her attention by filling her life with one problem after another? She should make everything a matter of prayer, but she didn't understand why God had allowed her to lose her job. Now this thing with Max didn't make matters easier.

Brittany closed her eyes and let a silent prayer form in her mind. *Lord, please forgive me for forgetting to rely on You. Please help me understand about losing my job, and help me deal with Max in a loving way. I need to know where to go from here. Please guide my decisions.*

High-pitched giggles caused Brittany to open her eyes. Entering the front door, Parker held a little girl under each arm, their dark braided pigtails hanging like ropes. "Hmm, where should I dump these sacks of potatoes?"

"Daddy, we're not potatoes," one of the little girls said through her laughter.

"You're not? I thought I had two sacks of potatoes." They wriggled to get down, and he set them on the floor.

"Daddy, you're too silly," the other child said as she stared up at him.

The scene stirred a myriad of emotions in Brittany as she remembered the way her dad used to play that same game with her and her brothers when they were kids. She tried to tamp down her reaction to Parker. She was letting emotions rule—not a good sign.

"Daddy, who's the lady?" One of the little girls pointed toward the loft.

"Hello, Brittany." Parker's gaze met hers. "Come on down, and I'll introduce you to Rose and Jasmine."

Embarrassed that she'd been caught eavesdropping, Brittany nodded and trotted down the stairs. The trio met her at the bottom. Eager curiosity painted the little girls' faces as they looked up at Brittany, yet they clung to Parker's arms with shyness.

"This is Rose." Parker tapped the top of the girl's head on his left, then tapped the one on his right. "And this is Jasmine."

"Hi, Rose and Jasmine. I'm Brittany." Brittany glanced from one child to the other and wondered how she would ever tell them apart. Heather had failed to mention that Parker's daughters were identical twins.

"I like your hair. It's pretty." Rose smiled shyly.

"Thanks." Brittany returned the smile. "I like your pigtails. Did you braid your own hair?"

The girls shook their heads in unison, their braids swinging. "Daddy did."

"Your daddy did a good job."

"Thanks." Parker's eyes twinkled as he hugged his girls and looked at Brittany. "I've had lots of practice."

Brittany took in the way Parker related to his little girls. Heather had been right. Their presence obviously brightened his life. Another piece of the puzzle fell into place, and Brittany had to admit that she was more intrigued than ever with Parker. Probably not a good thing when she suspected that Heather was trying to push her and Parker together. No matter how intriguing the man, the last thing she needed was a rebound romance.

Chapter Three

"Come on, Daddy. You have to come and play with us."

Parker turned away from the kitchen counter and toward the sound of his daughters' pleas. "Girls, I'm talking to Heather and your uncle John. You know better than to interrupt."

"But you guys never quit talking." Rose scrunched up her little face, her lower lip protruding.

Parker suppressed a smile and tried to look stern. "That doesn't mean you should interrupt, does it?"

"No." The girls shook their heads.

"So what do you say?"

"Sorry for interrupting," the girls replied in unison again.

"Good. Please remember that."

"We will. Are you going to play?" Jasmine waited for his answer, her dark brown eyes wide.

"Play what?"

Rose pointed toward the living room, easily visible in the house's open-floor plan. "Chutes and Ladders with Brittany. We need one more person."

Parker glanced over to see whether Brittany was watching, but she was talking with Heather's brother, Mike. A flash of envy sparked through Parker's mind. What a strange reaction—an uncalled-for reaction.

Before he could reply, Heather leaned over and whispered in his ear. "I think that's an excellent idea."

He turned and scowled at her. "I know what you're trying to do."

"Yeah, helping Rose and Jasmine find a fourth." Heather gave him a feigned smile of innocence.

"You're not fooling me." Parker stared at Heather and shook his head before he turned his attention back to his daughters. "Mike can be their fourth."

"Oh, no. Hannah and Lexi have already challenged Mike and me to play Rook." Heather grinned. "You see, the last time the cousins got together, Mike and I were the Rook champs, so they have to try to unseat us. We can't let that happen."

Parker tried not to frown. "Okay, I'll play."

"Yay!" Rose and Jasmine clapped.

"Calm down or I may change my mind."

With the little girls tugging on his arms, Parker trudged across the room. First Heather, now his girls. Was this a conspiracy to push Brittany and him together? Maybe he was being paranoid. The girls were too little to have any romantic ideas. They just wanted to play with their new friend. They'd practically adopted Brittany the moment they met her.

Parker tried to focus his attention on the game board sitting on the coffee table. He forced a smile as he surveyed the situation. Where should he sit? Next to Brittany or across the table from her? Either way, his mind wouldn't be on the game.

"Sit here." Rose pointed to the spot opposite where Brittany had taken a seat on the floor.

"Okay." Hoping to avoid looking at Brittany, Parker sat crossed-legged on the floor. "How do you play this game?"

Rose let out a huge huff. "Daddy, we've played this before. You should know."

"Oh, yeah, I remember now. I go up the ladders and down the chutes."

"That's right." Jasmine shoved the spinner at Parker. "We have to spin to see who goes first."

"Ladies should go first." Parker pushed the spinner back to Jasmine.

Jasmine giggled. "I'm a girl, not a lady."

Parker tugged on one of her braids. "You and your sister are little ladies."

Rose looked at Brittany. "And Brittany's a big lady."

"We say she's a grown-up lady, not a *big* lady."

Brittany chuckled. "It's not every day that someone calls me big. It's nice to be taller than someone for a change."

As the girls and Brittany laughed together, Parker couldn't help thinking about how the top of her head had barely reached his shoulder when she'd stood near him while they were skiing. There definitely wasn't anything big about the petite young woman sitting across from him, unless it was her heart, as she showed kindness toward his girls.

While his daughters took turns spinning, Parker finally ventured another look in Brittany's direction. She smiled again, and he couldn't deny the way it made his heart jump.

This was nuts. True, he hadn't associated with a single woman close to his age in a long time, so maybe his response was only natural. He was a man with an appreciation for a good-looking woman. That shouldn't bother him, except that he kept wondering whether she would make a good nanny for his girls. He was letting his need for a nanny run away with his thoughts.

Brittany took her spin. Tiny freckles dotted the back of her hand as her slender fingers flicked the little arrow, making it whirl around and finally land on the one. She looked up at him. "Well, *I'm* certainly not going first. Your turn."

"Okay." Parker reached for the spinner, and their fingers brushed. Her touch sent a jolt straight to his heart. He hoped the reaction didn't show on his face. Maybe it was her thoughtfulness toward Rose and Jasmine that had him feeling this way.

The arrow pointed to the number two.

"Yay!" Rose picked up the spinner. "I got the highest number, so I'm first."

"Yes, you are, and we'll go around the table this way." Brittany made a clockwise motion with her hand. "So your dad goes next, and I'm last, since I had the lowest number."

"But it doesn't always work out that way, does it, Daddy?" Jasmine looked at him for confirmation.

"No, it doesn't. Sometimes life isn't fair." Thoughts of the unfairness in his life threatened to darken his mood, but he wouldn't let negative feelings dampen this time with his girls.

Rose patted Brittany on the arm. "Daddy always says that when he tells us we can't stay up late, even though he does."

Nodding, Brittany chuckled. "Daddies are like that. My dad says that all the time, too, when I complain."

Parker didn't say anything, but wondered whether she was thinking about losing her job. He wanted his girls to grow up with a realistic outlook, though he hoped his sometimes-gloomy viewpoint wouldn't unduly color their world. Still, life wasn't fair. Sometimes it was downright unjust. There seemed to be a lot more chutes than ladders in his life.

As the game got underway, he tried to steer his thinking in a more positive direction. He was here with the family who loved him. That should be all he needed, but he sometimes wished he could have his old life back. That wasn't going to happen. Too much animosity still existed between him and the people he knew in Stockton, and he had to protect his girls from any unkindness. That was a top priority.

After each of them had a few turns, Brittany landed on a square where a ladder propelled her to a square near the top of the board. "Wow! I liked that spin."

"Now you're going to win." Rose stuck out her lower lip.

"You never know." Brittany shrugged. "The game's not over."

"Yeah. She could land on that chute a few squares ahead and go way back." Jasmine pointed to the place three spots away.

"That's true." Parker handed the spinner to Rose, so she could take her turn. He hoped her attitude improved. He hated dealing with her sour moods. Was it the result of the changes that had taken place on the ranch with Jenny and her family leaving, or had his less-than-sunny outlook rubbed off on Rose? He hoped he wasn't to blame. Being a parent held a lot of responsibility, but he was still glad for the choice he'd made to adopt these little girls.

"Daddy, it's your turn." Rose poked his arm with the spinner.

He took his turn, realizing he'd been doing too much thinking, rather than enjoying the game. When Brittany had her next turn, she landed on the square Jasmine had mentioned earlier.

As Brittany moved her game piece down the chute to a place much closer to the beginning, she laughed and gave Jasmine a playful tickle in the ribs. "How did you know that was going to happen?"

"It almost always happens when we play." Jasmine giggled.

Her high-pitched giggle joined Brittany's laughter. The joyous sound touched something deep inside Parker. It felt like the warmth of a sunbeam on a cold day, but he steeled his heart against it. He would let his little girls work on his emotions, but he couldn't let someone outside the family circle move him.

A little while later, Rose raised her arms above her head in triumph. "I won. I won."

Parker smiled at Rose. "Good job."

Brittany patted Rose on one arm. "You're the champ this time."

"I want to be the champ, so let's play again." Jasmine grabbed her game piece and plunked it down at the starting point.

Narrowing her gaze, Rose did the same. "Just cuz we play again doesn't mean you'll win. Maybe Brittany or Daddy will win."

"That's true." Brittany nodded. "But she's going to try, aren't you, Jasmine?"

"I am."

Rose tapped Brittany on the arm, then picked up the spinner. "I won, so I get to go first."

"That's right. You do." Brittany picked up her marker. "Let's get started."

Parker glanced over at Brittany. What did she think of his competitive daughters? Maybe he was too worried about normal sibling rivalry, but hadn't there been a lot more of it lately? That was another reason he needed to find a nanny. Isolated as they were, it was hard to gauge what was normal behavior. He needed another perspective.

Finally, the second game ended with Brittany as the winner. Parker reached over and put an arm around Jasmine's shoulders. "Well, Jas, looks like you and I weren't meant to be winners tonight."

"Let's play a different game." Jasmine glanced around the room. "Can we play cards like Heather?"

Before he could formulate a response, Brittany picked up a

deck of cards from the nearby end table. "Do you girls know how to play Crazy Eights?"

The little girls shook their heads.

"Then I'll teach you. It's easy. We'll play a practice hand to help you learn." As Brittany explained the rules of the game, she dealt out the cards, then with the cards exposed she showed them the strategies involved.

While Brittany helped Rose and Jasmine through the practice hand, Parker couldn't help noticing how well Brittany related to his girls. She'd welcomed their attention and had been patient with their bursts of temper.

When they finished practicing, Jasmine placed the cards in front of Parker. "Daddy, since you won the practice game, you can deal."

"Okay." Parker shuffled the cards.

He tried to soak up his daughters' joy while he dealt each person seven cards. But his thoughts didn't linger on the happy interaction humming through the room. For some reason, being around Brittany made Parker think of the twins' mother, Sydney. He didn't know why. Brittany didn't resemble Sydney in the least. Maybe it was the age. If Sydney were alive, she would be about the same age as Brittany. He'd tried to help Sydney, but he'd failed. All these years later, the failure still caused an ache deep in his soul.

While they played several games, Parker's thoughts kept coming back to the idea of asking Brittany about the nanny position. She fit seamlessly into his family circle. He had to talk to Heather about it.

"I've won two games in a row." Jasmine picked up the cards and started a clumsy attempt to shuffle them. "Daddy, you're not doing so good now that we're not playing a practice game. You need to pay better attention."

"Okay, I'll try." Parker chuckled, knowing that his mind had been preoccupied with Brittany, rather than Crazy Eights.

Rose turned her attention to Brittany. "How come you got those brown spots all over your face?"

A blush colored Brittany's cheeks, and Parker wanted to somehow take back his daughter's question. He didn't have a clue how to react to Rose's blunt observation. Should he apologize for Rose or try to make light of it? He hadn't thought about the fact that his girls had never been around anyone with freckles.

Brittany's laughter rescued him from his embarrassment. "The brown spots are called freckles."

"How come we don't have them?" Jasmine looked first at Rose then at him.

Again Brittany saved him from having to come up with an answer. "You don't have freckles because your skin has more melanin in it than mine."

Jasmine knit her eyebrows. "What's mela...nin?"

"It's a chemical that protects the skin from the sun." Brittany went on to elaborate about why she had freckles.

"I wish I had freckles like you." Rose gazed at Brittany with adoration.

Shaking her head, Brittany smiled. "You're the first person I know who wants to have freckles like me."

"I want freckles like you, too." Jasmine vied for Brittany's attention.

Laughing, Brittany gathered Rose and Jasmine in a hug. "You girls are wonderful. We all need to learn to be happy with the way God made us and not wish to be like anyone else."

The girls giggled, and Parker took in their joy. What did they think about the way Brittany talked about God with ease? Had he been wrong not to talk about God with them? He'd left that kind of talk to Delia and Jenny because he'd never resolved his own anger with God over what had happened with his job and Sydney.

As Brittany looked his way, he hated to admit that he was drawn to Brittany's cute freckled face, too. "Okay, girls, we're done playing games. Time for bed."

"No," the girls wailed in unison.

Parker stood. "Yes, you can play more tomorrow."

"Your dad's right. I'll even teach you some new games, okay?" Brittany gave the girls another quick hug, then glanced in his direction, seeking his confirmation.

"Sounds like a good idea to me." As Parker started to usher the girls toward the bedroom, he turned to Brittany. "Thanks."

"You're welcome. I had fun." Brittany waved.

While Parker led Rose and Jasmine up the stairs, he couldn't help thinking that he was looking forward to tomorrow, too.

With Rose and Jasmine tucked into bed for the night, Parker sneaked away to the pine-paneled room that was listed in the rental brochure as the owner's retreat. A small stone fireplace and a wall of bookcases filled with books of every description made for a cozy refuge. A dim glow emanated from a single floor lamp in the corner. The room offered Parker what he needed—a sanctuary and solitude. He liked the quiet because he was out of the habit of interacting with people.

As he settled on the recliner, a knock sounded on the door. Tempted not to respond, he sat there a moment and willed the intruder to go away, but another knock followed.

"Uncle Parker, it's Heather. May I come in?"

He couldn't help smiling. Heather knew him too well. She wasn't going to let him hide from his own guests. "Yeah."

Heather peeked around the door. "Do you have a few minutes to talk?"

Parker motioned for her to come in. "Sure. What's on your mind?"

"A couple of things."

Parker pointed toward the lounge chair on the other side of the rectangular dark pine table. "Make yourself comfortable."

"I heard you telling Dad at supper that Mark and Jenny left the ranch right after Christmas."

Sighing, Parker nodded. "Mark had an opportunity to run a bigger ranching operation in Colorado."

"Are you going to take over the ranch?"

"No, Derek is."

"What are you going to do about someone to watch Rose and Jasmine during the day?"

"I'm looking, without much success." Parker wanted to ask Heather about Brittany, but he hadn't had time to think the whole thing through. "I thought you were here to talk to me about something that's bothering you, not about my problems."

"They're sort of related."

"How?"

"I've been offered a research job in a small town near Boston, but I'm not sure about moving to the East Coast—so far away from anyone I know."

"I didn't know you had applied for a new job."

"I wasn't looking, but the company needs a nurse to work with a doc who is doing clinical trials. It's just what I want to do." Heather eyed Parker. "They want a decision by this coming Wednesday."

"You must want this position if you're thinking about accepting it without even seeing the place."

"When I was in middle school, we went to Boston on vacation."

Shaking his head, Parker chuckled. "I hardly think that

counts, especially since the job isn't in Boston itself. But it seems to me that you want this, so I say go for it."

"Then I need your help."

"What does this have to do with me?"

Heather grimaced. "My decision affects Brittany, and that's how this is connected to you."

Brittany. After the things he'd been thinking about her tonight, uneasiness hit Parker's gut. "What's the connection?"

"I'm worried about her. She doesn't have a permanent job, and I hate to leave her without a roommate. If I take the job, I plan to pay off my portion of the four months we have left on our lease. After that she'd have to pay all the rent by herself, and she can't afford to do that. I'm not sure whether I should take the job, or how I'm going to tell Brittany if I do."

"So what does this have to do with me?"

Heather looked down at the floor, not meeting his gaze. "I thought you could ask Brittany whether she'd like to have the nanny position."

Disquiet crept into Parker's mind, as he got up from the chair and walked to the window. He stared into the night. Light from the full moon shimmered across the snow. The moon was like a hole in the blackened sky and reminded him of the hole in his heart that nothing seemed to fill—even his little girls. How could he invite Brittany into his troubled life? But he'd already considered it. Heather was asking him to make a decision—one he wasn't sure he was ready to make, despite the pressing need for a nanny.

Turning from the window, Parker stared at Heather. "She's an accountant and a financial planner. Why would she consider being a nanny? That's a big comedown."

"The way I see it, you two need each other. You need a nanny, and she needs a regular job and a place to live. You can offer her both."

"This afternoon she mentioned something about moving

back to the Spokane area." Parker shook his head. "Besides, do you think she'd want to live on an isolated ranch? And how could she come live on the ranch when she's tied down with a lease?"

"I don't think she'll move back to Spokane unless she gets a job there." Heather narrowed her gaze as she appeared to be thinking. "As for the lease, you could pay her portion as part of your job offer."

Parker let out a harsh breath. "I could do that, but what would she think?"

"You won't know unless you ask." Heather shrugged. "Anyway, did you notice how Rose and Jasmine immediately took to Brittany?"

Parker didn't want to admit that he'd noticed, and he didn't want this to turn into another disastrous attempt to assist a young woman. Brittany would have to know about his past because he couldn't offer her the job in good conscience unless he told her about it. He wasn't sure he was prepared to do that. If he mentioned his reservations to Heather, she'd tell him to get over it, as she did every time she saw him. But somehow he couldn't let it go. The unfairness constantly ate at him.

"I hope your silence means you're considering my suggestion." Heather's statement interrupted his thoughts.

Hoping to avoid Heather's scrutiny, Parker looked out the window again. "Have you mentioned the position to her?"

"No. I thought I should talk to you first."

"Good." Conflicting thoughts raced through his mind. He wanted to help Heather, and he needed a nanny. So the decision should be easy, but the attraction he had to Brittany complicated the whole thing. "How will she react to my past?"

"I've mentioned it."

Parker's heart sank. He feared hearing about Brittany's reaction. "What did you tell her?"

Heather walked over and stood next to him. "She asked about Rose and Jasmine, so I told her about the rumors, about your losing your job and about Sydney's death."

"What did she say?"

Heather raised her eyebrows. "She said you were a very compassionate person and immediately believed you were innocent of any wrongdoing."

"That's good." Parker wasn't sure why he was so relieved.

Heather nodded. "Since you're going to ask her about the job, I suppose you should know I also told her you were a recluse because of what happened."

A recluse. No wonder Brittany had imagined him as an old man with a salt-and-pepper beard. "The recluse part's an overstatement."

"Not much of one."

Parker stopped himself before he tried to refute Heather's claims. Arguing with her would only put more ideas into her head. True, he'd kept to himself and rarely went into town. He didn't want to deal with the stares or whispered comments when he ran into people he knew—people who used to be his friends and coworkers. He didn't have anything to say to those people now, especially the ones from church. Why had they been so quick to condemn him? Where had God been in this mess?

Parker didn't have the answers.

Crossing her arms, Heather stared at him. "Since you seem to have lost your ability to talk, would you like me to run the idea by her?"

Heather's question rolled around in his mind. "I'll talk to her."

"She has great references." Patting herself on the chest, Heather grinned again. "Me. She's got experience as a substitute teacher, and she's terrific with kids, as you witnessed tonight."

Parker chuckled. "Have you ever thought of going into sales? You're very convincing."

"I just know how to make a persuasive argument. I say don't waste another minute." Heather pointed to the door. "Get out there and talk to her."

"You're not that persuasive. I'm going to sleep on it and see whether it still seems like a good idea in the morning."

"Hey, nerdly uncle, don't think too long, or I'll talk to her myself."

"Okay, nerdly niece, I've been forewarned." Parker couldn't help smiling at Heather's reference to him—a moniker that brightened his mood. They'd been teasing each other this way for years.

"You know you've got me beat in the nerd department. I always tell my friends that you're my mad-scientist uncle."

Parker turned to look at Heather. "Is that what you've told Brittany?"

"So you *are* worried about what she thinks?" Heather shot him a speculative grin.

Parker shook his head and gave Heather a wry smile. "I think you should go bother someone else."

"Okay, but while you're in here by yourself, why don't you spend a little time talking to God about hiring Brittany?"

Parker frowned. Why did Heather have to bring God into it? He hadn't helped before, so what reason was there to believe He would be there now? "You know my feelings about that, and they aren't going to change."

"I'm still praying for you. And so is the rest of the family."

Parker knew that was true. Every time he talked with his mother, he heard the same statement. "You always say that."

"I'm going to keep saying it until you get right with God."

"I gathered from something Brittany said tonight that she's a Christian, too."

Heather nodded. "We attend the same church. That's how

we started sharing an apartment. But don't let that stop you from talking to her."

"Your breathing down my neck is the only thing that'll stop me."

Heather backed up toward the door. "Okay, I'm out of here, so you can make plans."

"Thanks."

As the door closed behind Heather, he sank onto the nearby chair. Brittany seemed like an answer to a prayer, even though he didn't pray anymore. Was God working on him—pulling him in despite his resistance? Or were his thoughts getting way ahead of reality? Just because he asked her didn't mean she would accept.

Chapter Four

On Sunday evening, following an afternoon of skiing, Parker sat at the dinner table with his family. Although the sunny day had turned into a clear, cold night, the conversation and laughter around the table warmed Parker's heart. If he could capture this slice of happiness and take it home, maybe he could put the past behind him. That's the way he felt every year during this get-together, but the feeling soon faded. He hadn't learned to let go of the heartache or bitterness associated with his unfair treatment.

Parker looked across the table. Rose and Jasmine were laughing with Brittany and Heather. Their interaction reminded him that Saturday and Sunday's flurry of activities had never given him a chance to talk to Brittany. The whole weekend he'd watched her having fun not only with Rose and Jasmine, but also with the rest of his relatives. Brittany had charmed them all, including him.

Was that a good thing when he wanted to offer her a job? Doubts and questions floated through his mind.

As Parker finished eating, the jangling sound of a cell phone echoed through the room and interrupted his thoughts. He knew immediately who was receiving a call. That distinctive ringtone belonged to Brittany.

"Excuse me." Brittany jumped up from the table and grabbed her phone and a jacket. She answered the phone as she went out on the deck at the back of the house.

Picking up his plate, Parker tried not to appear interested in what Brittany was doing. "Delia, thanks for the great meal."

"Thanks. It was nothing." Delia waved a hand in his direction.

"Rose, Jasmine, let's help clean up." Parker motioned for them to follow.

Without protest, the little girls helped carry the dishes into the kitchen while the rest of the family also pitched in. As Parker loaded dishes into the dishwasher, he tried to ignore Heather. Every time he looked up she was staring at him.

Heather came up behind him and nodded her head toward the door leading to the deck. "Time's running out. I'll keep an eye on the girls so you can ask Brittany about the job."

Parker glanced out the window. Brittany paced back and forth across the deck as she talked on the phone. Her breath formed a cloud in the cold air—a cloud that matched the cloud of doubt forming in his mind. He wasn't sure about this, but he needed a nanny now so he could meet the deadline for his latest project. He needed someone to take care of his girls. "I can't interrupt her phone call."

"I didn't say you should. But as soon as she's finished—"

"I'll talk to her when she comes inside." Parker turned and looked out the window again as Brittany slipped her phone into her jacket pocket. She leaned her forearms on the railing and made no move toward the house.

"Looks like she doesn't intend to come in right now."

"Maybe she wants some time alone."

"No excuses." Heather smiled wryly. "I'll get your jacket, so you can join her."

Heather headed to the closet. Since she was on a mission, trying to stop her was pointless. After she returned, she handed him the jacket, then ushered Rose and Jasmine into the family room for a game.

Brittany continued to lean against the railing. Even in the dim light, her coppery hair shimmered. Putting on his jacket, he took a deep breath, then opened the sliding door. It made a whooshing sound as he closed it.

Brittany turned as he stepped toward her. "Hi. Sorry. I didn't mean to skip out on the cleanup."

"You don't need to apologize." Should he ask her about her phone call, or jump into the reason he was standing here in the cold? He shouldn't have let Heather push him into this until he was ready.

"That was my parents. They wanted to know how things were going." Brittany lowered her gaze and kicked at a chunk of ice that stuck to the floorboards of the deck. "I was hoping my dad had some good news about a job, but he found out that the position he'd mentioned to me last week has been filled."

"That's too bad. Do you have any other prospects?"

She looked up but faced away, her shoulders sagging. "No."

He shouldn't have been worried about how to approach his job offer. Her responses practically begged for him to ask her, but doubt made him hesitate.

"Did you want me for something?" She looked up at him, moonlight reflected in her eyes.

His pulse ricocheted in his head as he tried to figure out what to say. "Yeah, actually, I do."

"What?"

He could do this. "I need a nanny for Rose and Jasmine. Would you be interested?"

A little frown knit her eyebrows. Without saying anything,

she turned away from him and placed her gloved hands on the deck railing.

Had he totally insulted her with the offer? He joined her at the railing and looked out on the moonlit landscape. "Hey, I know this probably isn't what you're looking for, but—"

She turned abruptly. "I don't know what to say."

"Don't say anything until I explain what the job entails, and all the circumstances surrounding my girls and me. I know Heather told you some of the story."

"She did."

"I couldn't help their mother have a better life, but I intend to do everything in my power to make sure her daughters have a good life."

"Okay."

Parker turned back to the moonlit landscape. "Stop me if I repeat what Heather has already told you."

"Don't worry about it."

He gripped the railing and took in the snowcapped mountains barely visible in the distance. "Sydney, Rose and Jasmine's mother, was a smart young woman, but she came from a troubled home. I saw her potential when she was in one of my classes and wanted to help her, so I started tutoring her."

"Heather mentioned that."

"I thought if she did well, she could probably get a college scholarship, get away from her difficult family situation and have a chance in life."

"But she got pregnant."

"Yeah. She came to me at the beginning of her senior year and told me that she wanted an abortion, but I talked her out of it." Parker sighed. When he looked at those precious girls, he knew he'd been right to do so. But the heartaches that came with Sydney's pregnancy still troubled him.

"What about the father?"

"Not in the picture." Parker slowly shook his head. "She

pretty much indicated to me that she didn't know who the father was."

Brittany's eyes widened. "You mean Sydney was sleeping with more than one guy at the same time?"

"Probably." Parker nodded. "Her mother and stepfather used to be on the rodeo circuit, and their place was a flophouse for itinerant cowboys all the time. Who knows what went on there? Sydney didn't talk about her home life much. I always thought she did well in her studies because they were her refuge from the chaos in the rest of her life."

"Was there any cause to report the family situation to authorities?"

"There were never any signs of physical abuse, and I felt I would lose her trust if I meddled in her family life." Parker grimaced and shook his head. "I was hoping Sydney might confide in someone other than me, so I mentioned my concerns to a couple of her female teachers. But Sydney never opened up to anyone."

"Did you try to fight the school board's decision?"

Brittany's belief in him touched Parker's heart. "Yeah, in the beginning, but they'd made up their minds. I was tried and convicted without much of a chance to defend myself. The fact that I wasn't the father of her children didn't quell the rumors or the speculation, because Sydney couldn't name the man who *had* fathered her children. Everyone still concluded that I'd been sleeping with her."

"So what did you do?"

"Decided to quit fighting it and kept to myself on the ranch. I still stay away from Stockton, where I used to live and work. And I very seldom venture into Billings." Parker couldn't keep the resentment out of his voice. "Stockton's not that far from Billings, and I don't want to run into any of those people again."

"How did you come to adopt the girls?"

Parker took in Brittany's expectant expression and almost wished that Heather could have explained the whole story. But Heather didn't know everything. He had to do this himself.

Parker remembered the day Sydney had come to him for help. Looking at Brittany, he took a deep breath. "When Rose and Jasmine were almost a year old, Sydney brought them to the ranch and begged me to keep them there. She was afraid that her stepfather would harm them."

"Is that when you got them?"

"No. I tried to persuade her to let me take her and the girls to a women's shelter in Billings, but she wouldn't go. She told me she was afraid to leave her mother alone with her stepfather."

"Had she mentioned this problem before?"

Parker shook his head. "I knew people were coming and going at all hours of the day and night and that Sydney lived in a circus atmosphere, but I had no idea she was afraid of her stepfather or that he was violent."

"What happened then?"

"She shoved an envelope into my hand, then ran to her car and left. I couldn't stop her."

"What was in the envelope?"

"Her last will and testament—the kind you can make on the internet. She'd named me as the girls' guardian. It was quite a shock."

"So that's how you came to adopt Rose and Jasmine?"

Parker nodded. "But right then, I wasn't thinking about that. I was worried about her and those little girls. I immediately called the sheriff's office and asked them to check things at her house. A deputy went out there, but they found nothing wrong. So they couldn't do anything. Two days later Sydney's stepfather shot her as she attempted to wrestle the gun away from him. She was trying to protect her mother."

Brittany said nothing, only stared at him with sadness in her eyes. Laughter sounding from inside the house belied the solemn discussion outside.

"Of course, when I took in Rose and Jasmine and eventually adopted them, the rumors started again." Telling this story made him shiver more than the cold night air. "As I said, that's why I don't go into town."

"Don't people have other things to occupy their minds by now?"

"Maybe, but I don't want to take the chance that Rose and Jasmine might hear any unkind remarks." Brittany sounded like Heather and his family. They expected him to be over the thing that had turned his world upside down and inside out. But they'd never had to deal with the looks of contempt and derision he'd endured. He was in no hurry to interact with the people who had made that time of his life so difficult. Still, despite the troubles, he'd adopt the girls again in a nanosecond. "Rose and Jasmine mean everything to me."

"I can see that. What does the job entail?"

"So you're interested?"

"I don't know." Brittany shrugged. "I need a job, so I'll consider it, but I have to know what my responsibilities would be."

Parker didn't want to hope too much that she'd take the job, but he couldn't tamp down his expectations. He wasn't going to sugarcoat it. "I pay $600 a week, but that's negotiable. The hours are long—from eight in the morning until their bedtime, which is sometime between seven and eight in the evening. You have weekends off most of the time. You'll share lunch and supper with us except on the weekends when you're off, and since you'll be in the house where my ranch foreman and his family were living, you'll have your privacy in the evenings. The girls are homeschooled, so that will be part of your duties, too."

Her eyes growing wide again, Brittany shook her head. "I've only been a substitute teacher."

"You don't have to have a teaching certificate to homeschool. I can fill you in on their progress, and Jenny, who used to homeschool Rose and Jasmine along with her own kids, agreed to talk with her replacement. Besides, I've seen the natural rapport you have with the girls. That counts for a lot."

"But I'd feel inadequate."

"You have a college degree. You would do fine."

"Easy for you to say. You're a real teacher and know what you're doing."

"So does that mean you're not interested?"

Brittany took a deep breath while she contemplated her response. How could she consider this position when she'd vowed only days ago to get a real job that didn't involve kids? But Rose and Jasmine were adorable, and tonight had been fun. Was this an offer she couldn't refuse? "I'll have to think about it."

"That's fair." Parker stepped away from the railing. "When can you give me an answer?"

"The end of the week? Is that okay?"

"Sure."

"I need to pray about it. Will you pray, too?"

Parker narrowed his gaze as a muscle worked in his jaw. "You might as well understand that I'm not much of praying person anymore."

"You're not? But you went to church with us this morning."

"Yeah, I did, but I only attend as a concession to please my family. God and I haven't been on good terms for over six years, and one morning in church isn't going to change anything. Attending church makes me feel like a hypocrite."

"Oh, okay." Brittany stood there staring at him and wished she knew what else to say.

"Hey, don't worry about it. I have no quarrel with anyone else's relationship with God. I just haven't worked out mine."

"I'll pray for you, too." Brittany hoped she hadn't overstepped with her statement, but she wasn't going to hide her faith. She wanted to tell Parker that God was there no matter what was happening. She'd experienced some of the same doubts concerning God when she'd lost her job and things had gone sour with Max. In the end, she realized that good and bad things happened to Christians and non-Christians alike.

"Join the crowd." Smiling halfheartedly, Parker motioned toward the house. "They're always doing that, too. So far nothing's changed."

"But it will."

"You seem pretty sure about that."

"I am. I believe prayer works." Brittany made the statement to herself, as well as to Parker.

"You can pray all you want, but we'd better go back inside before we turn into icicles."

"Sure." Brittany chuckled, realizing that talking to Parker had made her forget about the cold.

He opened the door. "I'll get you one of my cards so you can contact me and let me know what you've decided."

"Okay." Brittany slipped past Parker and stepped inside.

Rose and Jasmine raced over before Brittany reached the living room. They each grabbed one of her hands. "We want you to play a game with us again."

Brittany gazed at the girls and wondered how she would ever tell them apart if she took the job. One more thing to consider when making her decision. "All right, as long as your dad says you can."

The twins immediately began pleading their case to

Parker, who smiled indulgently as he patted each one on the head. "You can play games until eight o'clock. Then it's time for bed."

Cheering in unison, they steered Brittany toward the coffee table where they'd set up a game of Sorry. As she moved to join the duo, Heather gave her a questioning look and walked over. While they settled around the table, Heather leaned over and whispered, "We'll talk later."

Brittany nodded. Was Heather behind Parker's job offer? Brittany suspected that she was. While they played the game, Brittany let the pros and cons of becoming Rose and Jasmine's nanny roll through her mind. Having a steady reliable income and a place to live would be big pluses, but living on an isolated ranch would definitely be a minus. Her father would consider this position a minus—a real negative as far as enhancing her resume was concerned. Then there was the matter of working with kids. She loved kids, but not when they were misbehaving. So far Rose and Jasmine seemed like delightful children. Still, weighing all these factors didn't help with her decision.

Despite her declaration to Parker that prayer worked, how was God going to let her know whether to take this job? She had to admit that sometimes God's direction wasn't always clear. But wasn't that what faith was all about—trusting God when there wasn't always a clear answer?

Rose came up to Brittany and gave her a big hug. "I wish you could come home with us."

"Me, too." Jasmine joined in the hug.

Brittany wondered whether the little girls' wish was God's way of letting her know that she should take the job. Rose and Jasmine had no idea that their dad had offered her the nanny position. She glanced at Parker. His expression told her that he was in agreement with his children, but, thankfully, he didn't mention his job offer to them. He was giving her time to make her decision.

"Would you like me to come for a visit?"

"Yay!" the girls chorused as they hugged her again.

Brittany watched their joy and realized that she'd invited herself without asking Parker. Hoping he understood her need to see the place where she might live and work, she turned to him. "Would that be okay?"

He nodded and gave her a big grin. "That's a good idea. When would you like to come out?"

"I'll have to let you know."

"I'll get that card, so you'll have all my contact information."

As the girls, Heather and Brittany starting playing the game, Parker disappeared. A few minutes later, he returned and laid a business card on the table near Brittany. He didn't wait for her acknowledgment but went to a nearby area where the men in the family were watching the football play-offs on TV.

While the others were taking their turns, Brittany studied the card, which listed Parker's phone and email contact information, as well as his occupation—medical writer. What did a medical writer do? Questions and concerns continued to churn through her mind during the two games of Sorry. At the conclusion of the second game, Parker appeared and announced that it was Rose and Jasmine's bedtime.

As he herded the girls toward their bedroom, Heather motioned for Brittany to sit next to her on the couch. "It's time for that talk."

Settling beside Heather, Brittany eyed her friend. "You have some questions to answer."

"Like what?"

"Did you put Parker up to asking me about the nanny position?"

"I didn't put him up to it. I suggested that he consider asking you." Heather leaned closer. "Did you agree?"

"I haven't decided yet."

"What's to decide? You need a job, and one has been dropped in your lap."

Brittany shook her head. "I'm not so sure I'm good with kids. I keep remembering that horrible group of fifth-graders."

"Rose and Jasmine aren't fifth-graders. They're two sweet little girls, and you've been getting along fine with them."

"I know they're your cousins, but even sweet little girls can be trouble." Brittany sighed. "Besides, I'm sure my dad will think it's not a wise career move."

"You're right. This isn't exactly what you were looking for, but it is a job. You can still keep an eye out for a finance position, but in the meantime, you'll have a steady paycheck. And I can personally say you'll have a very nice boss."

"I still have to consider all my options." Yes, Parker would make a nice boss. That was one of the problems, but Brittany wasn't going to mention it. She couldn't ignore the fact that she was attracted to him. He was a good-looking man and a wonderful father to those little girls. That was a powerful combination.

"You do, but I have something to tell you that might help you make your decision."

"What?"

"I have a new job offer."

"A new job? When did this happen?"

"I got the offer last week."

"Congratulations."

"Thanks."

Brittany knit her eyebrows. "But what does that have to do with my decision?"

"The job's in Massachusetts."

"Oh, so you'll be moving, and that's why you're pushing me off on your uncle?"

"I haven't made a final decision yet, but I'm very interested." Heather shoved a dark lock of hair behind her ear. "And I'm not pushing you off on my uncle."

"Then why didn't you tell me before now?"

"I was going to tell you, but when I got the offer, you had just broken up with Max. You were dealing with that trouble, and I couldn't bear to dump more bad news in your lap. Besides, I hadn't made a definite decision about taking it."

"So you tried to fix things by finding me a job?"

"No. I wanted to help both of you." Heather placed one hand on Brittany's arm. "Please don't be angry at me."

Brittany took a deep breath. "I'm not angry. Just feeling a little manipulated. That's all."

"I'm sorry. I didn't mean to make you feel that way." Heather shrugged. "I figured this was perfect. He needs a nanny, and you need a job."

"What about our lease? How will I get out of that?"

Heather shrugged. "I'm sure Parker can work something out for you."

"You mean like a loan?"

"Something like that."

As Brittany contemplated Heather's response, a loud roar of male voices sounded from the nearby room where the guys were cheering on their favorite football team. Brittany looked in that direction as Parker gave Heather's dad a high-five and settled on the couch next to him. "Guess they're having a good time."

"Yeah." Heather raised her eyebrows until they disappeared beneath her bangs. "Are you trying to avoid the current discussion?"

"No. There isn't anything else to say about it." Brittany shook her head. "I can't make a decision now. I told Parker

I'd have to pray about it, and I'd give him an answer at the end of the week."

"What did he have to say about that?"

Brittany proceeded to tell Heather about the conversation with Parker.

"Wow! I'm impressed that you got him to open up like that."

Brittany shook her head. "He doesn't need me to help him sort out his thoughts about God."

"Well, no…but maybe your presence on the ranch will—"

"Don't talk like I've already agreed to take the job." Brittany lifted one hand as if stopping traffic.

"I know you don't want to hear this, but I can't help thinking that you'd be wonderful for Parker. He needs someone to rescue him from the past, and I think you can do it."

Brittany opened her mouth to protest. "But—"

Heather held up both hands in front of her. "Hear me out. I didn't invite you on this trip for any reason other than to help you get your mind off Max and your job situation. I wanted you to have some fun. But when I walked into the restaurant at the ski lodge and saw you and Parker engaged in conversation, the thought that you two would make a great couple just popped into my brain."

Brittany shook her head. "Not a good idea if I'm working for him."

Heather put a hand over her heart. "It would be like a fairy-tale story—like *The Sound of Music* without so many kids."

"You are a dreamer." Brittany rolled her eyes. "And I'm done talking about this."

"Okay, I won't say another word about it; but, like you, I'm going to pray about it."

"Thanks." Brittany hugged Heather, then sat back and looked at her friend. "Can you tell the twins apart?"

"Sometimes." Heather chuckled. "You should've been

around when the girls first came to live with Parker. He painted one of Rose's toenails in order to tell them apart."

"Does he still do that?"

"I'm not sure, but if you notice, Rose always wears something red, and Jasmine always wears something yellow. Does your question mean you're seriously thinking about taking the job?"

"I'm asking questions to help make that determination." Grabbing her purse from the floor, Brittany stood. "I'm going to call my parents and ask for their advice."

"If they tell you to take the job, will you do it?"

Brittany smiled. "Has anyone ever told you that you should go into sales instead of research?"

Heather laughed. "Yes, as a matter of fact. Parker said so the other night."

"When you were badgering him to hire me?"

Heather gave Brittany a playful shove. "Go talk to your parents and follow their advice."

After talking with her parents, Brittany had no more answers. They'd hesitated to tell her what to do. They helped her talk through the situation, but they told her that they couldn't make the decision for her. She lay on the bed and stared at the ceiling. If only God could write the answer on the ceiling as he wrote on the wall in the Old Testament story of King Belshazzar. Of course, she didn't want an ominous message to appear, but a clear-cut answer would be nice.

But maybe God was giving her an answer in all the things that were falling into place. She needed a permanent position, and one had been offered to her. She would need an affordable living situation because she was almost certain that Heather would take this new offer. Housing was provided with the nanny job. Rose and Jasmine were adorable little girls. Did these things outweigh her misgivings? Maybe a trip to the ranch would answer those questions.

Chapter Five

The following Wednesday afternoon, Brittany tromped across the snow-covered ground as she tried to match Parker's long strides. Rose and Jasmine, bundled up in hooded coats, mittens and boots, skipped ahead toward the one-story house with bright blue shingled siding. It sat between the big house, as Parker called it, and the gray pole barn on the right. Outbuildings and a couple of other small houses with roofs covered in snow dotted the nearby acreage.

Snow clung to the bare branches of the trees surrounding the house, and icicles, hanging from the eaves, sparkled as they melted. Everything in sight glistened in the sunlight. Brittany squinted at the brightness. Was the dazzling sunshine an indicator that she should take the job? She hated to keep looking for signs, but she wanted to make the right decision.

Parker stomped the snow from his boots as he unlocked the door, then pushed it open for her to enter ahead of him. "Well, this is it. I lived here while I was growing up and right before I finished the big house, which was built after they discovered oil and gas deposits on the land."

Brittany glanced around the modest little house, taking in the stone fireplace in the living room and imagined Parker sitting in front of it when he was a little boy. She shook the thought away. She needed to concentrate on Rose and Jasmine and her reason for being here, not think about Parker. But he was a part of the equation she couldn't ignore.

As he took her on a tour of the cozy three-bedroom house, she wondered whether the oil and gas deposits were the reason Parker could afford to take his family on ski vacations every year. Rose and Jasmine's chatter accompanied them as they went from room to room, allowing Brittany to observe rather than converse.

"Here's the schoolroom." Again Parker stepped aside so she could enter first. "Jenny set it up while she was home-schooling her kids and my girls."

While Brittany took in the two computers sitting on computer desks along one wall, Rose grabbed one of Brittany's hands and pulled her farther into the room until she was standing next to a light oak-colored school desk. "This is my desk, and that one is Jasmine's. We're learning lots of math. Daddy gave us our lesson this morning. He's been teaching us since Miss Jenny left."

"See where we practiced our lessons?" Jasmine pointed to the white board standing on an easel in the corner. "Computers are fun, but I like to write on the board."

Brittany nodded. "Looks like you girls are doing well in your math lessons."

Rose tapped Brittany on the arm. "Are you going to be our new teacher?"

Expectation infused those words and the expressions on the faces of the two little girls. How could she say no? But she couldn't make a decision because of two cute little girls. She had to weigh the pros and cons. She glanced at Parker and he gave her a wry smile, making her stomach do one of those roller-coaster dives. She wasn't sure whether the cause was her impending decision or his smile.

Parker stepped over to the desk. "Girls, if you don't bug Brittany and you stay on your best behavior, that'll help her say yes."

"We'll be real good, won't we, Rose?"

"I'm going to be very good." Nodding, Rose looked over at Brittany. "I even made my bed and helped Delia clean our room today."

Brittany patted Rose on the back. "Good for you."

"Now will you say yes?" Jasmine tugged on Brittany's coat sleeve.

Rose frowned at her sister. "Jas, we're not supposed to bug her."

"Oh, I forgot." Looking at Brittany wide-eyed, Jasmine slapped a mitten-covered hand over her mouth.

Brittany pressed her lips together in an effort not to laugh.

"Okay, girls." Parker put his hands on their shoulders. "Brittany and I need to talk about some things, so I want you to go back to the house and help Delia. I saw some towels that needed folding."

"Are you coming to the house when you're done?" Rose stared up at Parker.

"We will."

Jasmine sidled up next to Parker. "Can Brittany eat supper with us?"

Parker glanced up. "Can you stay?"

"Please, please, please." Jasmine and Rose jumped up and down and clapped, their mittens making a dull thud as their hands met.

"Thanks. I will." Brittany didn't have the heart to say no, even though she didn't relish the idea of driving home after dark in her unreliable car on the unfamiliar country roads. But eating with them would help her see what life would be like if she were to live here.

"Okay, then that's settled. Run along and tell Delia we'll have one more for supper."

The girls scrambled to beat each other to the front door. Brittany watched them through the living-room window as they held hands and meandered through the snowdrifts on their way back.

"Sometimes, when the girls do something or say something they shouldn't, I have a hard time keeping a straight face while I'm disciplining them."

Brittany turned to see Parker standing behind her. "I'm so glad you told me that. I was trying so hard not to laugh at their antics."

"I want to make sure they don't make any major detours. As you can see, they aren't exactly taking a straight path to the house." Parker joined her in front of the window as they returned their attention to the little girls' trek through the snowy yard.

"They're certainly having a good time." Parker's nearness made her heart thump, and she mentally put that fact on her list of negatives. Could she take this job when she had an attraction to the boss?

They watched Rose and Jasmine until the girls finally entered the rustic log house that sat on a knoll overlooking a snow-covered meadow and the Beartooth Mountains in the distance. If she took this position, the view out her window would always be spectacular. She had to put that fact in the plus column.

Parker turned to her. "Thanks for understanding their excitement. They really want you to be their new nanny."

"Yeah, I guess I'd have to be pretty clueless not to know."

"Well, what do you think? Have they convinced you?"

And what about you? The phrase flitted through Brittany's mind. Thankfully, she hadn't voiced the thought aloud. Brittany held a smile in place, hoping that her thoughts weren't transparent. Did he think she was a good choice or was he desperate and doing Heather a favor?

As the questions tumbled around in her thoughts, Brittany was beginning to realize that her ego had taken a big hit when she'd lost her job and an even bigger hit when Max, more often than not, chose his studies over her. Now her self-esteem was at a low point that found her wishing Parker showed as much enthusiasm about her taking the job as the girls did.

"Does your silence mean you're going to turn us down?"

"It means I haven't made up my mind." Brittany continued to stare out the window. She didn't want to look at him for fear that he could tell how his nearness made her insides a jumble.

"Seems like I need to do some more selling, then."

"You said you wanted to talk to me. About what?" She hoped some conversation would help her gain her equilibrium.

"I wanted to tell you a little more about the girls and the ranch and what you can expect to do as the girls' nanny."

"Is this part of your sales pitch?"

He smiled wryly. "Yeah, if you want to look at it that way."

"Okay. I'm listening."

Parker pulled a sheet of paper from the pocket of his coat and handed to her. "Here's an approximate schedule that they keep, including the time they get up and when they go to bed."

Brittany looked over the paper. "What about discipline? Would I correct them or leave that up to you?"

"If you were to see the need to discipline them, you would do so. If you waited for me to do something about their misbehavior, then the disciplinary action would lose its impact."

"Your preferred method?"

"Time-outs work great for them or losing privileges.

They're really good kids. They like to compete with each other, but in the end they are each other's best friend."

"I can see that." Brittany smiled. "Anything else I should know about the ranch?"

"Sure. Derek Johnson runs the ranch now. He and his wife, Christine, have a two-year-old boy and another one on the way. They live in one of the other houses on the property just down the lane from here. We also have three hired hands who live in the bunkhouse on the other side of the machine shed."

"I know you told me that you don't work the ranch, so why do you live here if you don't do any of the ranching?"

"While I was growing up, I did enough work on this place to know that I didn't want to do this for a living. It's a hard life, but some people love it, and I'll gladly pay them to do it."

"Why keep it?"

"I like seeing the cattle roam this land. Since the ranch has been in my family for four generations, I hated the thought of it passing out of our hands. None of us kids were interested in running the operation. Mom and Dad were getting too old to handle the ranch, even with hired help." Parker chuckled. "Maybe someday I'll have to make this a dude ranch where people can come and pretend to be cowboys."

"So you like living here."

"I do. When that bad business with Sydney came up, this ranch was the perfect place for me to live."

A perfect place to hide. Brittany didn't say it, but the thought sprang to mind. Heather's suggestion that Brittany could rescue Parker from the past also flitted through her brain. Is that what she'd be doing if she came to work here? She wondered how Parker spent his days. She'd never gotten around to asking him about his work as a medical writer.

Now would be a good time to elicit that information. "Your card says you're a medical writer. What does that mean?"

"I write a lot of articles and papers for doctors and nurses, who have done research projects and need someone to write a report for them. I write and design newsletters and continuing education manuals. It's a good fit for me with my science background."

"You like it better than teaching?"

Parker hesitated. "It pays a lot better."

Brittany didn't miss the hitch in Parker's voice. The money might be better, but she had no doubt that he missed teaching. "Why don't *you* homeschool Rose and Jasmine now?"

"I've had fun the past couple of weeks teaching them, but I also came to realize that I can't do the medical writing and do a good job of teaching, too. Besides, with Jenny homeschooling her kids, it was a natural fit for the girls when they were ready for school." Parker stared at her. "And they need more than a teacher. They need someone to watch them while I'm busy working. I'd like that someone to be you. Rose and Jasmine need you."

"I still have to think about it." Brittany swallowed the lump that suddenly rose in her throat. If the choice was only about Rose and Jasmine, the decision would be easy. But the fact that her boss would be a handsome man who made her heart trip gave her pause. Her heart was still so fragile after everything that had happened with Max. She didn't think she could handle developing feelings for a new man who was even more emotionally unavailable.

"So I haven't convinced you yet?"

Brittany shook her head. "I can't make a decision right this minute. And I have one qualifier. If I do agree to your offer, I want to continue to look for a job in my field. Even though my dad didn't say one way or the other whether I should take this position, he did say that if I did, I should keep that option open."

"I can live with that." Parker walked to the front door and put his hand on the knob. "Let's head over to the big house. Maybe Delia's mouthwatering beef stew will entice you to accept."

Lights glowing in the windows made an inviting picture as Brittany followed Parker. She tried not to examine the disappointment that flickered in her thoughts because he'd so readily accepted the fact that she wasn't interested in something permanent here. But when Rose and Jasmine greeted her at the door with smiles and hugs, Brittany knew she was going to accept the position even though Parker's presence sparked emotions that were better left unexplored.

The following Monday, Parker stood on the porch of Brittany's new home and surveyed the ranch that was covered in a blanket of fresh snow. Thankfully, the storm had only minimally affected the cattle, and the snow hadn't altered her plans to move her things from Billings to the ranch. With help from Derek and the ranch hands, the move went without a hitch.

Parker waved as Derek made his way to his pickup. Parker had invited Derek and his family, as well as the hired hands, to supper, but they all had plans for the evening. That meant having to entertain Brittany by himself unless he counted Rose, Jasmine and Delia. But the girls would go to bed early, and Delia would make herself scarce as soon as the kitchen was clean. That would leave Brittany and him alone. The thought left him uneasy.

He didn't want to be an ungracious host on her first night at the ranch, but after he'd practically begged her to take the job, he was having second thoughts. Not because she wouldn't make a wonderful nanny, but because he couldn't stop thinking about her. Ever since she'd accepted the position, the image of her cute freckled face kept popping into his head. Maybe the reality of having her here would put an end to that. He wished.

"Daddy, Daddy, come see how we're helping Brittany." Rose poked her head out the front door.

"Okay, but let me take off these wet boots."

"Hurry."

Parker had purposely spent most of his time loading and unloading the furniture and boxes outside. He'd let the other guys take things inside. That way he could avoid being around Brittany. He figured that once she was settled he wouldn't have much reason to interact with her on a regular basis. She'd have her work, and he'd have his. Then he wouldn't think about her so much. Was he kidding himself?

Trying not to examine that question, he padded through the house in his stocking feet. He followed Rose to the kitchen where Brittany and Jasmine were hunkered down beside a box that sat on the floor. They were taking the packing paper off dinner plates and stacking them on the nearby table.

"See how much we've unpacked?" Rose pranced around the room pointing out the empty boxes.

"I do." Parker glanced at Brittany, who looked up just at that moment. Their eyes met. His heart thudded. He ignored it. He wasn't going to let her pretty face turn his head and make him wish for something that couldn't be. She was his employee, and any romantic notions were completely off-limits. Besides, she wasn't here permanently, and that suited him just fine. "You need another helper?"

Brittany stood and pointed to a group of serving dishes sitting on the counter. "You'd be a big help if you put these things on the top shelf. I'm too short to reach it."

"No problem." As Parker placed the items on the shelf,

he tried not to think about how her simple request filled him with satisfaction. When he finished, he turned around. "Anything else?"

She smiled at him. "Thanks. I think that's it."

Her smile seemed to turn his stomach inside out. He was in deeper trouble than he thought. "Is all your furniture where you want it?"

"Yeah. The guys did a great job."

"Good. Guess there isn't anything else for me to do except relieve you of these boxes, unless you want to keep them."

"Oh." She turned to look at the jumble of cardboard at one end of the kitchen. "I'll keep a few. Where do you suggest that I store them?"

"The basement. Tell me which ones you want to keep, and I'll take them down for you."

Brittany pointed to several, and Rose and Jasmine helped him carry those to the basement. After he was done, he stopped near the kitchen doorway. "Unless you have something else you want me to do, I'll head back to the office. Call if you need anything."

Brittany looked at Rose and Jasmine, then back at him. "Do they need any lessons today?"

Shaking his head, Parker knew he'd made the right decision to hire Brittany. She placed Rose and Jasmine's welfare first. "Delia took them through their lessons today."

"And she said we were well-behaved." Rose puffed out her little chest.

"Good job." Parker patted the girls on the head. "Now I want you to be well-behaved for Brittany."

"We will, Daddy. We're going to be a big help." Jasmine reached out and gave him a hug.

"I know you will." He hunkered down and brought both girls into a group hug.

Rose looked up at him. "Daddy, don't forget. Brittany needs a hug, too."

Hug Brittany. Parker's heart nearly stopped at the thought. What should he do? Was a quick brotherly hug in order? Unfortunately, his thoughts about Brittany weren't exactly brotherly, but she didn't know that, did she? His mind buzzed, and he couldn't think clearly.

As if she understood his dilemma, she stepped forward and put one arm around his waist, then immediately stepped away, giving him basically what he'd call a half hug. "Thanks for your help."

"Sure. It's the least we could do."

"When should we come over?" Brittany stood between the girls with her arms resting around their shoulders.

"Whenever you want. The girls can show you around, if you'd like." With a wave, he put on his boots, then raced to his pickup.

As he drove along the snow-packed drive, he hoped Brittany didn't regret taking this job. Even after Rose's embarrassing suggestion, part of him still wished he could stay, but another part wanted to get away as fast as he could. Although he didn't need to rush back to work, he needed to go for his own sanity. Maybe time away would enable him to get his head on straight.

The delectable aroma of Delia's chili filled the house as Parker stood by the floor-to-ceiling window. The pole light near the edge of the drive illuminated the yard and made the snow glisten, despite the dim light of the setting sun. As Brittany, Rose and Jasmine made their way toward the house, their long shadows danced across the glimmering whiteness. Brittany said something, and the girls giggled, their breath sending clouds into the cold air.

He loved to watch their happiness. Already Brittany was a

part of that. Despite the unsettled feeling she brought into his life, he was glad she was here. He would get used to having her here. He hoped.

The sound of little high-pitched voices drew his attention to the interior of the house. He looked toward the kitchen where Delia stood by the cooktop, stirring the chili. Just off the kitchen he could see the mudroom where boots, coats and mittens went flying as Rose and Jasmine took off their outerwear.

He drew closer. "Girls, you know better than to leave your things lying on the floor. What should you do with them?"

"Hang them up," they replied in unison, then hurriedly gathered their belongings from the floor.

"That's right." Brittany glanced up at him. She looked fantastic in her slim jeans and off-white cable-knit sweater, but he wasn't pleased with himself for noticing. "Please show Brittany where she can hang her coat."

The little girls pushed past each other, trying to be the first to lead Brittany to the nook off the mudroom. When they came back into the kitchen, Brittany greeted Delia as Rose and Jasmine raced over to him.

"See what I made?" Jasmine thrust a little booklet with a yellow construction-paper cover at him.

A second later Rose gave him one with a red cover, but she was hardly able to hold still. "Open it. Open it."

"I'll open them after we sit down together. Let's go in here." Parker motioned to the den.

Parker settled on the brown leather sofa with Rose and Jasmine on either side. Brittany sat on the nearby rocking chair. He tried to keep his attention on the little booklets in his hand rather than on Brittany, but he couldn't help noticing how she sat on the edge of her seat as if she were waiting for his approval.

He handed the booklets back to the girls. "Whose turn is it to go first today?"

"Jas's." Rose's shoulders slumped.

"Okay." Parker patted Rose on the arm. "Don't look so sad. You know I'll look at yours, too."

Rose sat up straighter as Parker took Jasmine's booklet and opened it. One page contained a drawing, and on the opposite page was the beginning of a little story. He looked over at Jasmine. "Would you like me to read it?"

"Yeah." Jasmine snuggled up close to him.

Before he started to read, he looked over at Brittany. "Your idea?"

Nodding, she gave him a tentative smile. "They worked on them while I was putting things away."

He nodded his approval, then began to read. After reading Jasmine's story about a lost dog that was found, he read Rose's story that also featured a dog—one that could sing. They had their mother's imagination and talent. She'd been a gifted writer. He wished he had some of her stories to share with her daughters, but all of that was gone.

Sadness surrounded his heart, but he fought against it. His girls were happy, and he would be happy, too. He put his arms around their little shoulders and pulled them close. "You girls did a super job. We'll have to put your stories on a bookshelf in here."

After the girls put their books away, he turned. Brittany stood there looking on as if she felt out of place. He wished he could take away the lost look on her face. Was she having second thoughts about taking the job?

"Chili's ready." Delia's voice sounded from the kitchen.

Rose and Jasmine raced ahead. Parker motioned for Brittany to go first as they left the den.

She turned to him. "Thanks for making a big deal out of their little books."

"No thanks needed. Are you settled?"

"Almost. I love the built-in hutch in the living room."

"My mom had a plate collection she used to display in there. She collected souvenir plates from the places she visited."

"I put my dog collection in it."

"Dog collection?"

"Yeah. I have these different dogs—stuffed, ceramic, plastic, knit—all kinds of them. I wanted a dog when I was a kid, but my mother's allergic, so we couldn't have one."

"That's too bad."

"Anyway, my dad gave me this cute stuffed dog for my birthday one year to take the sting out of not getting a real dog. Then every year after that, he got me a different dog of some kind. Pretty soon relatives and friends were giving me dogs of every description for special occasions. I have some unique ones in my collection."

"Sounds interesting. You'll have to show it to me sometime."

"I will. I think my collection inspired Rose and Jasmine's dog stories." Brittany chuckled.

When Parker and Brittany entered the kitchen, Rose and Jasmine were already seated at the rectangular pine table. Their legs dangled from their chairs. Delia placed a large blue tureen in the center of the table.

Brittany looked his way. "Where would you like me to sit?"

"I want her to sit across from me." Rose pointed at the chair opposite her.

"No, she should sit across from me."

Parker stared at his children and hoped they didn't start a big quarrel. "No arguing, girls. We have our system. Jasmine got to read her book first, so Rose gets to choose where Brittany sits."

Rose started to cheer, but Parker gave her the eye. She stifled her cheer and sat politely while Parker pulled out the chair opposite Rose for Brittany.

Delia settled in her spot and looked at the girls. "Whose turn to give thanks for the food?"

Rose's hand shot up. "Mine."

As Parker bowed his head, he didn't miss Brittany's puzzled expression. Would she ask him why he didn't pray but the girls did? Or was she too polite to inquire?

After the prayer, Parker dug into his chili. The girls chattered and giggled with Brittany and Delia. And despite his worries about what Brittany might say or do, he drank in the lively sounds. Having her at his table added a new dimension to his household, and he was afraid he was enjoying it way too much.

Chapter Six

Parker turned off the kitchen light as he said good-night to Delia. "Okay, girls, we need to take Brittany on a tour of the house. I hope your room is clean."

"Daddy, you know it is. You told us yesterday that we had to clean up for Brittany." Rose scrunched up her face.

"But that was yesterday. I wasn't sure about today." Parker winked.

"We made our beds and everything." Looking up, Rose grasped Brittany's hand. "Come and see it."

Not to be outdone, Jasmine took Brittany's other hand. "This way."

Brittany let the girls lead her down a short hallway while Parker followed close behind them. When they came to a door on the left-hand side, the duo led Brittany into the room.

She stopped and took in the twin beds with the simple slatted-pine headboards, matching chests and child-size desks. "Your room is very neat."

"Thanks." Rose pranced over to her bed. "Do you like my ladybugs or Jas's dragonflies better?"

The curtains and comforters had a light green background. Rose's comforter was covered in red and black appliquéd ladybugs while Jasmine's was dotted with yellow and black appliquéd dragonflies. "Oh, I like them both. Did you pick them out?"

Rose nodded. "Delia helped."

While they toured the other parts of the house, Brittany realized that those oil and gas deposits on this ranch must have put substantial deposits in Parker's bank account. The main floor sported four bedrooms and three-and-a-half baths besides Delia's gourmet kitchen with the latest appliances and conveniences. The tongue-and-groove knotty pine vaulted ceilings and beams added a Western flavor that fit the Montana location.

Rose pulled on one of Parker's arms. "Daddy, show her where you live."

Parker laughed. "You make it sound like I live in a different house."

"But you live on a different floor."

"I live in the whole house, but I sleep and work in the basement. I think my room is clean, so I can give you a tour." Parker winked again.

Brittany's stomach did a little somersault. He was getting to her again. "Sure. Lead the way."

While Rose and Jasmine escorted Brittany to the stairs, she kept picturing some kind of cave-like dwelling in the basement. She banished the image from her mind. She was letting Heather's description of Parker as a recluse color her thoughts. Parker was not a hermit, or at least not one with no social interaction at all. He had his family.

When they reached the landing at the bottom of the stairs, Rose and Jasmine sprinted around the corner. Still trying to wipe away the image of a cave from her mind, Brittany peered into the room. This was no dank, dark basement. The place looked like something out of an interior decorating magazine.

"See what Daddy has down here? His own kitchen." Rose hopped up on one of the stools at the snack bar.

Jasmine joined her. "Do we get a snack?"

Parker leaned against the counter in the galley kitchen. "How about some popcorn and a movie, then bedtime?"

"First let's show Brittany the rest of the basement." Rose jumped down from the stool and raced through the galley kitchen.

While Brittany followed the trio, she took in the large adjoining room. It contained a pool table, a large-screen TV and a sectional covered in a brown tweed fabric. When the girls said their dad lived on another floor, they weren't far from the truth. Was this where Parker locked himself away from the rest of the world?

Jasmine hurried to a door on the far wall and opened it. "Here's Daddy's office."

Both girls darted through the door, and Parker strode after them. "Girls, you know you're not supposed to go in there without me."

Jasmine rushed back through the doorway and sidled up to Parker.

Rose looked back around the doorframe. "But you're right behind us."

"I know, but rules are rules."

Rose moved into the doorway and stomped a foot. "I don't like rules."

"Then maybe you'd like to sit out here while Jas and I show Brittany my office."

Not daring to move, Brittany took in the exchange and wondered whether this was the kind of thing she would have to deal with. Up until now, both Rose and Jasmine had been fairly well-behaved other than a little sibling rivalry. She should have known better. Suddenly the job seemed a lot harder than she'd anticipated if she had to deal with Rose or

Jasmine's defiance of adult authority. Was she going to be sorry that she'd agreed to be their nanny?

Brittany held her breath as she waited for Rose's response.

The little girl scrunched up her face as her lower lip protruded. She clomped over and stood in front of Parker, her arms crossed. "Okay, I'll wait for you."

"Good. We can go in together." Parker glanced over at Brittany. "Ready?"

"Yes." Curiosity propelled Brittany to hurry as she followed Parker. What did he have in here that prompted him to make the place off-limits to his daughters unless he was with them?

"This arrangement works out very well for me since I often work late or get up early. Being down here, I don't disturb anyone with my unusual hours." Parker patted the speaker with several knobs and buttons located on the wall by the door. "And we have an intercom system, so anyone can reach me. And during the night, it monitors the girls' room in case they need me or Delia."

"That's super." While Brittany took in Parker's explanation, she couldn't help feeling that he was justifying his basement existence. But maybe she was imagining his almost-guilty description of the gadgets in his living quarters.

"We can talk through the intercom, and it even plays music." Seemingly having forgotten her earlier scolding, Rose pranced around Parker as if she couldn't contain her excitement. "Show Brittany how it works."

"Not now. I'll show her later. You girls want to see your movie, don't you?"

"Yeah." They jumped up and down and clapped their hands.

"Then let's go." Parker flipped the switch, turning on the lights in the room ahead, then stepped aside so that Brittany could go first.

She entered the huge room with knotty-pine paneling and a couple of Native American prints on the wall. Desks, computers and bookcases loaded with books and binders filled the space. He opened a door on the right side of the room and flipped another switch. A burst of light came from the fluorescent fixtures and illuminated what appeared to be a workshop with work benches, tools of every description and all kinds of other paraphernalia. No wonder Parker didn't want his girls in here without him—too many things for little hands to break.

Jasmine tugged on one of Parker's arms. "Daddy, tell her about your invention."

"You have an invention?" Brittany remembered Heather's reference to her mad-scientist uncle. Was this the reason?

Parker grinned. "Let's say I'm tinkering. I've been experimenting with ways to use waste from the ranch to produce fuel for heating and running some of the machinery. It's a work in progress. I've been studying some of the methods used by other people and trying to make something that will operate here."

"That's impressive. Do you have something that's functional?"

"Not yet. I'm still testing things." Parker led the way back into his office. "So now you've seen where I spend my time."

"You have plenty to keep you busy." Brittany wondered whether he ever missed interacting with people.

"I do." Parker looked at the girls. "Are you ready for that movie?"

"Yay! It's my turn to pick." Jasmine dashed through a doorway at the other end of the kitchen.

Parker glanced at Brittany. "You can help them pick out a movie while I make the popcorn."

"Okay." Brittany followed the girls to a doorway off the kitchen area.

Brittany reached the doorway and stopped. She was sure her mouth was hanging open. The room was like a mini-theater with a movie screen that covered one whole wall. At least a dozen chairs, covered in plush navy blue upholstery, filled the open area in front of the screen. No wonder Heather considered her uncle a recluse. He never had to go anywhere. He could send the hired help for supplies, and everything else he needed was right here in this house—even the entertainment.

Did this isolation have a negative effect on Rose and Jasmine? So far Brittany hadn't seen any, but more time with them would give her a better idea. She glanced back at Parker. "Your own movie theater?"

"Yeah. Heather's dad and I built it and installed the sound system. That's John's field—electronics. We did a lot of our own finishing work in this house, too. My dad was a real handy guy, and he taught John and me a lot about construction."

"That's wonderful."

"My sisters did most of the decorating. My family is welcome any time to share in this house. But they have busy lives and don't get here as often as I would like."

Brittany was tempted to tell him that he could visit them, but that would be unwise. She had to keep those kinds of opinions to herself. "They did a beautiful job. Your house is lovely."

"Thanks. Later, when I show you how to work the intercom, I'll teach you to operate everything in here, so whenever you have educational videos to show the girls, you can use the theater."

"Sounds like I have as many lessons to learn as they do."

Parker opened a cupboard and grabbed several bags of microwave popcorn. "If you ever have any questions, don't be afraid to ask."

"I won't." Brittany knew there were some questions she didn't dare ask. "I'll see what movie the girls have picked out."

While Brittany watched Rose and Jasmine go through the library of DVDs stored in a bookcase, she thought about trying to keep the girls straight. Thankfully, Heather had clued her in on the red and yellow color scheme that Parker had adopted. But now she was beginning to see a subtle difference in the two girls. Rose was definitely the more outspoken one. She appeared to take the lead most often. Even now, although it was Jasmine's turn to pick, Rose was exerting her influence.

"I picked one." Waving the DVD case in the air, Jasmine ran over to Brittany. "Do you like this movie?"

Brittany looked at the case. "*Babe.* I love the story of that little pig. He's so cute. Good choice."

Rose stepped in front of Jasmine. "I helped, too."

"What did they choose?" The smell of popcorn accompanied Parker as he appeared in the doorway with the snacks.

"*Babe.*" Rose grabbed the DVD and held it up.

"Okay. Find your seats, and I'll set up the show." He gave each of the girls a juice box, then handed the bags of popcorn to Brittany. "If you want something to drink, there's plenty of pop in the fridge."

After Brittany got her drink, Rose and Jasmine jostled to sit beside Brittany, who wound up between the two girls. In a minute the lights in the room dimmed and the movie began.

After Parker sat in a chair directly behind Brittany, he leaned over and whispered, "Looks like you're the most popular girl in town. Everyone wants to sit by you."

Does that include you? The question slipped into her mind. She squelched it immediately. She couldn't let romantic feelings about Parker enter her head. He was her employer, and this was only her first day. Somehow she was going to have to keep these wayward thoughts in check. Somehow.

Throughout the rest of the movie, the girls giggled and clapped at the appropriate times, and Parker made silly comments that made his daughters giggle even more. Brittany sat back and took it in. How sad that this man who cared for these little girls and his family had cloistered himself away in this house—magnificent as it was. Heather's words popped into her mind. *He needs someone who can rescue him from his past.*

Brittany wasn't sure she wanted to rescue him or whether she could. She'd been hired to take care of two little girls, not help their father. She put that thought squarely in her mind.

The movie came to an end with rousing cheers from Rose and Jasmine. Parker suspected that a few tears welled in Brittany's eyes while the credits rolled. She was trying to hide the fact that she was wiping her eyes, so he didn't want to bring it up and embarrass her. Her reaction to the happy ending reminded him that she had a tender heart. He'd guessed that by the way she spoke about her family and even her old boyfriend and the way she treated Rose and Jasmine.

"Okay, girls, you know what time it is."

"Do we get a story even though we had a movie?" Jasmine asked sidling up to him.

"A short one."

"I get to pick. It's my turn," Rose announced as the twins scrambled up the stairs.

"Brush your teeth," Parker called after the girls, then turned to Brittany. "Would you like to read the story?"

"I can. Is this one of my nightly duties? Although I don't consider it a duty, but a pleasure. I wanted to make sure I don't intrude on your parenting time with the girls."

Parker realized that Brittany was trying to find her way in

this new job, and she obviously didn't want to overstep her bounds. He needed to set her mind at ease. "Some nights I work late and just run up for good-night kisses and hugs. On nights when I'm not working late, I'll be there for storytime."

"Oh, that's good to know." Brittany smiled brightly as if to cover her nervousness.

After Rose and Jasmine got ready for bed, they sat on Rose's bed for the story. Parker lounged against the door-frame as Brittany read. She made the characters come alive. The girls were enthralled. Every new thing he learned about Brittany made him realize that he'd made a wise decision in hiring her, even though her presence more often than not made his pulse beat a little faster. He couldn't let himself be interested in a young woman who was working for him and one who didn't intend to stay long-term.

Brittany finished reading the book, then closed it. Parker stepped into the room as the girls went to their respective beds and slipped under the covers. After tucking them into bed and giving them hugs and kisses, he turned out the over-head light, leaving a princess night-light glowing in the dark-ened room.

"Good night. See you in the morning."

"'Night, Daddy. 'Night, Brittany."

"Good night." Brittany's soft voice sounded in the dimly lit hallway. "Do you want to show me how to operate every-thing now?"

Parker shook his head. "I'll do it tomorrow evening after supper. Doing the intercom now wouldn't work with the girls already in bed."

"Oh, of course."

"Do you have any other questions?"

"Yeah. How do you keep track of whose turn it is?"

"You mean with Rose and Jasmine?"

Brittany nodded. "I think my mind was spinning tonight with the whole 'It's my turn' stuff."

"I don't keep track." Parker chuckled. "It's impossible."

"How do you make it work? Don't they ever argue about it?"

"So far, since we've started this system, it seems to be self-policing. They keep track." Parker shrugged. "I know someday a disagreement is bound to happen, but I'm not going to concern myself until it does."

"Well, I hope it doesn't happen on my watch." Brittany shuffled toward the kitchen. "I guess I'd better be going. Thanks for the tour and the movie."

"If you don't mind staying awhile longer, I have some things I'd like to explain to you."

"Oh, sure. That's fine." She looked at him, her expression radiating curiosity.

Parker wanted her to understand everything about his children. But he didn't know whether he had to do that explaining now or whether he was asking her to stay because he didn't want her to go yet. He didn't want to examine his reaction to her departure too closely.

"What do you want to tell me?" She stood there looking a little uncomfortable—like an employee who'd been called in for a talk with the boss.

"Would you like a cup of coffee while we talk?"

Brittany shook her head. "I don't drink coffee."

"How about hot chocolate?"

She smiled. "Sure. I'd like that."

"Then hot chocolate it is." He led the way into the kitchen. "I hope you don't mind the instant kind. Microwaves are my favorite cooking appliance."

Chuckling, Brittany sat on one of the stools at the center island. "I don't mind. That's how I usually make it."

While he waited for the microwave to heat the hot chocolate, he leaned against the counter. "Marshmallows or no marshmallows?"

"Marshmallows."

The microwave beeped. Parker set the steaming mugs on the counter and plopped several miniature marshmallows into the hot liquid, then gave one to Brittany. "Let's drink it in the den."

"Okay." Brittany followed him into the cozy room.

"Have a seat." He picked up a remote from the coffee table and punched a button. Instantly, flames danced behind the glass in the fireplace built into the wall opposite the sofa.

"That's an easy way to start a fire." Kicking off her shoes and tucking her legs up under her, Brittany settled on the sofa as she took a sip of the hot chocolate.

"The wonders of propane."

"If you get your invention to work, would you be able to use it to run this fireplace?"

"Possibly. I think the success of that invention is a long-time coming." Parker laughed halfheartedly. "It's my hobby. If something comes of it fine, but if not, there's no loss."

"But it must be somewhat important to you. Rose and Jasmine were very eager for you to tell me about it."

"Yeah. They're little kids and impressed by some not-so-impressive things that I do."

"They love their dad. That's obvious."

"It humbles me to know that." Parker knew their love made his life worthwhile. They softened his heart—a heart that had grown cold with bitterness. The love and trust of his family had kept him going during his darkest days, but Rose and Jasmine gave him that feeling every day. Yet the bitterness lingered. He couldn't shake it.

"So what do you want to talk about?" Her coppery hair gleamed in the firelight.

Parker grabbed hold of the sofa arm to keep himself from

reaching out to touch it. He needed to think about the girls instead of the young woman sitting near him. He took a deep breath. "I wanted you to know that Rose and Jasmine's grandfather was a Crow Indian. As part of their studies, they've had some simple lessons on the Crow Indian tribe, so they know a little about that part of their heritage."

Brittany frowned. "You're talking about Sydney's father, not her stepfather, right?"

"Right. Sydney's dad was killed in a rodeo accident. From what I understand, her life was pretty good until her mother married again when Sydney was about ten."

"Do the twins ever have contact with their grandmother?"

Parker shook his head. "She's never made any attempt to see them in all the years I've had them. She moved away after her husband went to prison, and I've never heard from her again."

"That's kind of sad."

"Yeah, it is, but in some ways it makes things simpler. I don't have to make any explanations."

"What would you do if she showed up one day and wanted to see the girls?"

"I would gladly let her see them, but I have no idea where she is or how to contact her."

"What do Rose and Jasmine know about their mother?"

"They know she died when they were babies, but not how. I have a few photos from the high-school yearbook that I've shown them. That's about it. I wish I had more." Parker took a deep breath, then glanced over at Brittany. "Someday I'll have to tell them the whole story because eventually someone, somewhere, will tell them, if I don't. I'm not looking forward to that day."

"I'm sure you're not. My heart aches for both you and your kids at the prospect of having to bring to light that horrific event."

"Not one of my favorite topics." Parker took a swallow of his hot chocolate, then placed the mug on the coffee table. His eye caught the little books the girls had made. They would be a much better topic of conversation. "I noticed the colors of the girls' books. Did you know about the color scheme we've been using to tell them apart, especially at a distance?"

Brittany nodded. "Heather told me. Have they ever tried to trick you by switching clothes?"

"Not that I'm aware of, but I'm pretty sure I could tell them apart now even if they did."

"Now that Jenny and her kids have left, do you ever worry that your girls will feel the lack of playmates and social interaction with other kids?"

"Not much. Homeschooling suits us here because it means they don't have to spend hours riding a school bus, and they don't have to face any unkind remarks."

"I have a friend from high school who homeschools her kids, and she's involved with a homeschooling association. Is there one around here that organizes field trips and stuff like that?"

"There's one in Billings, but that's an hour away. Although last fall Jenny took the kids to one event sponsored by a homeschool group. They went to a museum in Billings."

"What about church? Do Rose and Jasmine go?"

Parker raised his eyebrows. "You know I don't take them."

"I'd like to go to church and take the girls."

Parker picked up his mug and took a long drink. He didn't want Rose and Jasmine anywhere near the people in Stockton. There were five churches in that little town, and the leaders in all of them had spoken against him. No one from any of the congregations had come to his defense, not even the people he considered his good friends in the church he'd attended at the time. Everyone turned away.

Brittany's eyes widened. "I didn't mean to overstep in

asking. I thought the girls would enjoy going to the children's classes."

Parker released a harsh breath. "I don't care what you do as far as church attendance is concerned, but I don't want Rose and Jasmine to go and hear something unkind."

A puzzled frown covered Brittany's freckled face as she shook her head. "I can't believe someone would say anything unkind about or to those sweet little girls."

"Well, I'm not taking a chance." Drinking the last of his hot chocolate in one gulp, Parker got up. "Do you have everything you need over at your place?"

"I'm fine." Standing, she picked up her loafers. "I want to make sure. You said there's no need for me to come here in the morning. You'll be sending the girls to my place for class at eight?"

"That's right."

Brittany held up her shoes. "Is it okay if I leave these in the nook where the kids keep their coats and boots, so I don't have to cart them back and forth?"

"Sure. You can leave anything over here that you might need."

"Thanks." She smiled, but it looked forced.

Parker stood there, an awkward silence spilling around them. "Would you like me to walk you home?"

She shook her head, the uneasy smile still curving her mouth. "No, thanks."

"I'll at least walk you to the door." Parker followed her to the nook.

She shrugged into her coat without saying anything. Finally, she looked up. "Good night."

"Good night." He opened the door for her, then watched as she trudged across the stark white landscape.

He didn't turn away until she entered the house and a light came on inside. He returned to the den to retrieve the mugs.

Brittany's sat there half-full. Shaking his head, he closed his eyes against the evidence of his rude behavior. After a pleasant evening, they'd ended on a bad note. That's not the way he'd intended their talk to go, but he had to protect his daughters.

Now Brittany probably had a negative opinion of him. Maybe, in the end, that was a good thing. He didn't need the distraction of something that might tempt him to spend time away from his work. He had an all-important deadline to meet. That's where his priorities lay. Future contracts depended on it. Besides, all this would protect him from his own heart—the heart that threatened to betray him by finding a little corner where feelings for Brittany could reside and undermine his determination not to open his heart again to any woman.

Chapter Seven

Snow still covered everything in sight as Brittany stood at her living-room window and watched Rose and Jasmine. They danced their way across the distance between their house and hers. With each step, they kicked up snow that sparkled in the sunlight. Their breath formed clouds as they laughed.

Brittany's stomach twisted with nervous anticipation. She didn't know why she was worried. Everything should be fine. The lessons were ready, and she'd had no trouble with Rose and Jasmine yesterday while they'd helped her unpack.

As the duo drew nearer, Brittany went to the door and opened it. "Hi, girls. How are you this morning?"

"Good. Delia made pancakes for breakfast. They were yummy." Rose took off her boots and put them on the mat near the door. They left a little puddle as the snow clinging to them immediately melted in the warmth of the house.

"Daddy ate five." Jasmine blew out her cheeks like a chipmunk. "He must've been hungry, but I'll bet he's really full now."

"I guess so." Brittany helped the girls hang up their coats, hats and gloves while she tried not to think about Parker. Her focus had to be on the two little girls, who were hopefully eager to learn. "Let's go into the schoolroom."

"Okay." Rose raced ahead.

When Brittany and Jasmine reached the doorway, Rose had already turned on her computer. Brittany didn't say anything but stood there with her hands on her hips and stared at Rose. Would the child eventually turn around and realize that she'd barged ahead without permission?

"Rose, you didn't ask Brittany if you could turn on the computer." Jasmine's words dripped with superiority. "You're going to be in trouble."

Brittany waited for Rose's reaction to her sister's comment.

Rose turned around. "Miss Jenny didn't care if we turned on the computer."

"Most of the time the computers were already on because Emma and Josh were already using them." Jasmine looked first at Brittany, then back at Rose.

"So?" Rose jutted out her chin.

"So you girls can start out at your desks this morning." Brittany took a deep breath, let it out slowly and hoped the girls would do as she said.

Brittany wondered whether she was going to have to deal with the Rose from the other night—the one who didn't like rules. Was the child going to test her authority right from the start? Was this going to be substitute teaching all over again?

Rose narrowed her gaze. "I don't want to sit at my desk. I want to stay here."

Jasmine went to her desk, then looked at Rose. "I'm going to tell Daddy that you didn't obey Brittany."

Brittany resisted the urge to put her fingers to her forehead to rub away a burgeoning headache. She didn't want Jasmine tattling to Parker. Brittany knew she had to handle this on her own or she would appear incompetent. Maybe she was. No, she couldn't think like that or the kids would sense it.

"Jasmine, thanks for going to your desk. I appreciate that." Brittany decided to ignore Rose for the moment and hoped that would prompt her to go to her desk, too. Brittany had discovered while substitute teaching that often ignoring students' misbehavior took the potency out of their schemes to upset her.

After grabbing a pencil and pad, Brittany sat on a chair near Jasmine. "I'd like for you to help me make some rules for our classroom."

"Okay." Jasmine nodded her head and took out a pencil and paper.

"This is the first rule. When you come into the classroom you should go to your desk unless I tell you to do something else, okay?"

Jasmine nodded. "Should I write that down?"

"We can both write it down." Brittany wrote a number one on her tablet, then printed "Sit at desk" in bold letters, and Jasmine copied it.

Rose still didn't move from the computer, but Brittany refused to look directly at the child. She hoped this wouldn't turn into a battle of wills—one that she was afraid she would lose.

"What's next?" Jasmine tapped her pencil on the desktop.

"That's not how Miss Jenny did it." Rose walked to her desk but didn't sit. "We could do whatever we wanted when we came in. I wish Miss Jenny and Emma and Josh were here."

Brittany smiled, hoping Rose couldn't tell that the statement had bothered her. Why was Rose being so uncooperative? She'd been as eager as Jasmine to have Brittany as their nanny. Rose's behavior made no sense, and Brittany had no idea how to deal with it, other than to pretend it didn't perturb her. "I know you miss your friends. It's hard when friends move away. I'll miss Heather when she moves."

"Me, too." Jasmine nodded. "She's going really far away, isn't she?"

"Yes, but we can talk with her on the phone, and if you girls are really good, we can talk with her on the computer, so we can see her."

"I wanna do that." Jasmine turned to Rose, who had been strangely quiet during the conversation. "See why you have to be good? We won't get to see Heather on the computer if you aren't."

Frowning, Rose crossed her arms. "I don't care."

Brittany tried to think of a response that wouldn't show her frustration. "Okay, then Jasmine and I will talk to her if you don't want to."

Rose didn't say anything. She just maintained her miffed stance. Sadly, even bribes weren't working. Maybe that wasn't the best way to get Rose to cooperate anyway. Brittany continued to make a list of classroom rules with Jasmine.

While Brittany and Jasmine worked, Rose's demeanor still didn't change. Brittany wondered whether she should somehow give Rose a chance to save face, but Brittany didn't know how to do that. Nothing came to mind. Her first day, and it was turning into a disaster. What had she gotten herself into? Had she made the wrong decision about taking this job?

What if Parker walked in on this mess? Who would be in more trouble—Rose or her?

After Brittany and Jasmine finished the simple list of rules, Brittany grabbed a book from the nearby shelf and held it up. "Let's start out this morning with a story. This is *No Children No Pets,* a book about a family who visits Florida so they can see the apartment building they've inherited. My mom read this to me when I was a little girl."

"Miss Jenny never started by reading to us." Rose stepped closer to where Brittany stood. "Besides that sounds like a dumb story."

"I'm sorry you feel that way." Brittany swallowed hard and hugged the book to her chest as if it could shield her from Rose's complaints. "I know this isn't the way Miss Jenny did things, but give this new way a chance."

Shrugging, Rose pressed her lips together and crossed her arms again.

"If that's the way you want to be, you can stand there, or you can go to your desk and sit down." Brittany opened the book.

Jasmine waved a hand in the air. "I want to try the new way. I like to hear stories."

"Thank you, Jasmine." Brittany took a deep breath and began to read.

Rose slowly made her way to her desk and slipped into her chair. Brittany said a silent prayer of thanks as the little girl laid her head on her desk. At least she'd quit complaining.

Brittany read the first chapter, then closed the book and put it back on the shelf. "We'll read another chapter tomorrow. Now we'll do our spelling lesson."

Rose lifted her head. "But that's not—"

"Not the way Miss Jenny did it." Brittany gazed at Rose and hoped for some kind of breakthrough. How was she going to proceed with the daily lessons if one of her students wouldn't cooperate?

"Will you read some more of that book?" Jasmine's question drew Brittany's attention away from Rose. "I want to hear more. Please?"

"Me, too." Barely audible Rose's words gave Brittany hope for the rest of the day.

"Okay." Brittany hurried over to the bookcase and retrieved the book, glad that she'd taken the time to check out a number of children's books from the Stockton library. She started to read again, hoping this would solve the problem with Rose, at least for the time being.

After Brittany read two more chapters, she closed the book again. "Okay, we have to do our other lessons now."

"Will you read first thing tomorrow?" Rose asked. "I liked the part about trying to fry eggs on the sidewalk."

"Me, too." Brittany smiled with relief. One hurdle conquered. Hopefully, there wouldn't be many more, but something told Brittany that this wasn't the last one.

On the following Monday evening, Brittany stood in the doorway to Rose and Jasmine's bedroom while Parker tucked them into bed. During the past week, Brittany had taken in this scene numerous times, then returned to her little house without discussing the situation concerning Rose. Every time Brittany thought about talking to Parker, she chickened out. She didn't want to feel like a failure after the first week on the job.

Brittany tried not to think about how she still hadn't made a connection with Rose, who did all her lessons but without much joy or interaction. Thankfully, Jasmine volunteered to answer every question, making the lesson time at least tolerable.

Although they'd made it through the first week, Brittany held her breath every evening, waiting for one of the girls to tell Parker how badly things were going in their classroom. But they never said much about their lessons, and Parker never asked. He often seemed preoccupied. Brittany wasn't sure whether to be thankful for that or not.

Despite the less-than-ideal teaching atmosphere that Brittany faced each day, the girls' arrival each morning was a welcome relief from the lonely nights she spent in the little house. She occupied her evenings by searching the internet for job opportunities and preparing resumes, but the job front was discouraging. Teaching was discouraging. Everything about her life seemed discouraging.

Something had to change.

Maybe she wasn't the person who should tell Parker how to deal with his kids, but somebody needed to tell him that things weren't good. She couldn't forget the statement Rose had made at the close of their lessons on Friday. A glower dominating her expression, the little girl had said, "Since you came here, Daddy doesn't play with us anymore. He works all the time. I wish you'd go away."

She didn't know how he would take it. But tonight, when Parker had chosen to continue working during dinner rather than sharing the meal with his little girls, Brittany decided that she couldn't worry about what might happen to her position here. Rose and Jasmine's welfare was more important than her job.

She kept reminding herself that God was in control. He would see her through this troubled time, but she had to address the problem no matter what the consequences. So she'd decided to face her fear and talk with Parker. He needed to know what was going on with his children. Would he welcome her concern?

Because Parker had already paid off her part of the lease, she'd put off this confrontation, knowing he could fire her. If he did, she would somehow have to pay him back, but she couldn't let things go on this way.

Brittany joined Parker in the hallway after he said his final good-night and switched off the light. "Do you have a couple of minutes to talk?"

He turned and looked at her in the hallway's dim light. "Sure. What's on your mind?"

This was it. She couldn't let cowardice win now, but self-preservation almost had her saying *never mind.* She took a deep breath. "I need to talk to you about Rose and Jasmine."

"What about them?"

"Well, mainly Rose."

"Rose, huh? Is she being too bossy?" He chuckled and motioned toward the den. "We can talk in here."

Parker sat on the couch and stared at Brittany as she took a seat on the nearby chair. "So what has Rose done now?"

Despite his lightheartedness, his scrutiny curdled her stomach. Had he expected this report? Had the girls said something to him over the weekend? He didn't seem concerned that Rose might be acting out. Brittany twisted her hands in her lap, unable to meet Parker's gaze. "Rose doesn't seem to be adjusting very well to my being here."

He narrowed his gaze. "What do you mean by that?"

Before Brittany had a chance to change her mind, she launched into an account of Rose's actions during the week.

"I see." Parker paused, but Brittany didn't look up and he went on. "The girls have been fighting with each other on and off since Jenny left."

Brittany finally had the courage to look at Parker, and he wasn't smiling. She swallowed a lump that had formed in her throat. "That's not exactly the situation here. They have been getting along with each other, but Rose doesn't want to cooperate with me. She seems so different from the little girl I met on the ski trip or even the one I visited here before I took the job."

Parker shook his head. "Don't worry about it. She'll get used to the new routine."

"I think there's more going on here than getting used to my routine."

"What?"

Brittany stared at the floor. Did she dare say what was on her mind? "Maybe it's not just Jenny leaving, but your working so much, too."

"So you think I'm not spending enough time with my kids?" The beginnings of a scowl furrowed his brow.

Shrugging, Brittany wondered whether she'd overstepped

the bounds of her position. Well, if she had, she might as well step in all of the way. "Think about it. After Jenny left, you took over their lessons until I arrived. Then you went on the ski trip and spent a lot of time with them. I arrive, and suddenly you spend nearly all your waking hours in your office."

"I have a job to do that's taking a lot of time right now. It's not always this way."

"But maybe right now your girls need a little extra attention from you."

"So, what are you suggesting?"

Brittany had no answer to his question. Big help she was. "Nothing."

"Are you trying to tell me that you can't handle the job?"

Brittany's stomach sank. Was he going to fire her? "No, I can handle it." She hoped. "I wanted you to be aware of the situation."

He gave her a stern look. "Rose can be a handful at times. So you have to be firm."

"Okay." Brittany wondered whether she should even bring up the visit to the library, but she knew there was something Rose loved—books. "One more thing."

"What's that?"

"I'd like to take Rose and Jasmine into Stockton, let them get library cards and check out some books."

A frown clouded Parker's handsome features. "In case you forgot, I don't have much use for that town. I'm not letting you take them anywhere in Stockton so they can be the subject of stares and gossip."

"Did you ever think that keeping them isolated on this ranch isn't good for them?"

"Going to Stockton is what's not good for them." Parker narrowed his gaze. "If they need books, buy them on the internet. I have a special credit card I use for school supplies."

"But that's not the same as going to the library and learning to pick out your own books." Brittany wished she could tell him that he was being unreasonable, but that would accomplish nothing. They were at a stalemate. "I hope you won't live to regret your decision. You can't keep them out of Stockton forever."

Parker didn't say anything for several seconds, just continued to stare at her. Brittany's pulse thundered in her head. What was he going to do? He abruptly turned and strode down the hallway toward the kitchen. Brittany scrambled to catch up. She was afraid to speak as he opened a cupboard and pulled out an expandable file folder.

He rifled through it, then held out a plastic card to her. "Here. I should have given this to you before, but I was thinking you probably had all the supplies you needed. Guess I was wrong. Buy some books and whatever else you need."

"Thanks. I will." She would order the books, but she wasn't going to give up on persuading Parker that he was wrong to isolate his children.

The clack, clack, clack of the keyboard echoed in the otherwise silent room. While Parker worked, another sound intruded on his thoughts. He stopped for a moment and listened. Someone was knocking on his door. The girls and Delia knew that the "Do Not Disturb" sign tacked on his door meant exactly that unless there was an emergency.

Was Brittany his visitor? He'd never mentioned the sign to her or its importance. If he ignored it, would she go away? Almost two weeks had gone by since their disagreement about the library. Was she here to badger him again about spending more time with his children? She had to understand that he had obligations to his clients. And he'd hired her to take care of his children, so he could do this work. He'd been avoiding her because he didn't want to see the disappointment in her eyes when he refused to go along with her ideas about Rose and Jasmine.

The knock came again. Parker sighed. Turning in his swivel chair, he looked at the door. She would be on his mind whether she left or not. He'd already lost his train of thought, so he might as well answer it.

Before he reached the door, it eased open and Brittany poked her head around it. She grimaced as she stared at him. "I know your sign says not to disturb you, but I have something important to tell you."

He motioned for her to come in. Despite being irritated with the interruption, he smiled. Although they were at odds concerning Rose and Jasmine, even their disagreement didn't diminish his attraction to Brittany. Her presence still brightened his day. "What is it?"

"Two things." She held up two fingers. "Valentine's Day is this coming Tuesday, and Rose and Jasmine made Valentines for you and Delia today. They are so excited about them that they couldn't wait to give them to you. So you really need to be there for supper tonight. And they've planned a tea for lunch on Valentine's Day. So please set aside an hour or two for their party, but don't tell them I told you. They made invitations and wanted to surprise you tonight at supper, but I was afraid you'd be holed up down here and not join us."

He held up a hand. "You can come up for air now. I understand."

She shrank back toward the door. "I'm sorry. I didn't mean to go on and on, but I wanted you know their plans."

"Gotcha. I'll be there. When Delia has supper on the table call me on the intercom, and I'll be right up."

"'Bye. Thanks." Flashing him a big smile, she waved and quickly left the room.

Parker turned back to his desk, but he couldn't concentrate. Brittany was on his mind. She'd seemed almost scared to interrupt him. Did she think he'd be angry that she wanted to talk to him about the girls' plans? He hadn't meant to seem intimidating or unapproachable. Was that how Brittany saw him? Or the girls? He remembered what Brittany had said about the way he'd been with Rose and Jasmine before Brittany came to work. Did his daughters think he didn't have time for them now?

True, he'd been swamped with this project and spent most of his waking hours on it, but he hadn't intended to ignore the girls. He just figured that the less time spent with Brittany, the less chance there was that she was going to soften his heart further.

Getting back to work was imperative. He had a client to please and a deadline to meet, but his kids were more important than either one of those. Brittany had made him see that he'd become a detached father. If necessary, he'd stay up late and get up early to complete the project, so he could be there for Rose and Jasmine.

During the rest of the afternoon, he anticipated hearing from Brittany, but when the call came, Jasmine's sweet little voice sounded over the intercom.

"Daddy, we're ready to eat."

What bad timing. Parker looked at the chart he was about to load into the report. He didn't want to stop before he finished. He held down the talk button. "Hi, Jas. Can you give me five more minutes? Then I'll be right up."

The intercom crackled, then he heard Brittany's voice. "Five more minutes. That's it. If you're not up here by then, I'll come down there and turn off your computer."

"Okay. The teacher has spoken, and I'd better get my work done before she takes away my gold stars."

"I don't give gold stars—only smiley stickers."

He heard giggles in the background.

"Okay, I'll expect a smiley sticker in five minutes."

Right from the beginning she hadn't been afraid to speak her mind. One more thing he liked about her. One more thing that made him think about her too much. While he put the chart into the document, his mind buzzed with thoughts of Brittany.

As soon as the chart finished loading, Parker jumped up from his chair and sprinted to the stairs. He took them two at a time. He hit the top step with fifteen seconds to spare. When he entered the kitchen, Brittany, Delia and the girls, who were already seated at the table, turned to look at him.

"Daddy, you made it. Now you get a smiley face." Jasmine bounced in her seat.

"We're having lasagna." Rose pointed to the casserole dish in the middle of the table. "I know you like it lots."

"I do." Parker pulled out his chair. "Should I serve?"

"We have to pray first." Rose folded her hands.

"Oh, that's right. Are you going to pray?" Parker cocked his head toward Rose.

"It's my turn." She bowed her head. Parker bowed his head, as well, and for the first time in a long time, he didn't feel like a hypocrite when he did it. Maybe those prayers that Brittany had talked about were starting to work on him. He wasn't sure how he felt about that, but maybe, as Heather often told him, God hadn't given up on him. When Rose finished saying her prayer, he raised his head and Brittany was looking at him, a speculative gleam in her eye.

He grinned at her. "Are you going to give me my smiley-face sticker now?"

"I don't have any with me." She laughed.

He let the sound wash over him and settle around his heart—the one that she was slowly thawing. He reminded himself not to get too attached. This wasn't the job or the life she wanted. But he couldn't deny his feelings for her were growing.

"Daddy, you can get your smiley sticker when you come to our party." Jasmine shoved an envelope at him while Rose handed one to Delia.

"A party?" Parker ripped open the envelope and pulled out a white card covered in heart stickers and the printing of a six-year-old scrawled across it.

"Can you come?" Jasmine leaned forward in her chair, anticipation written all over her face.

"We're going to make you lots of good stuff." Unable to contain her excitement, Rose wiggled in her chair.

"I'll be there. Thanks for inviting me."

Delia set her invitation beside her plate. "Thank you, girls. I'm looking forward to your tea. Now let's eat some lasagna."

"Wait. We have something else for you." Rose held out another envelope to Delia and to Parker.

Jasmine produced two envelopes, as well. "Valentines for you."

"Is it all right if I wait until Valentine's Day to give you yours?" Parker knew that would be a necessity. He hadn't even thought of Valentine's Day because he'd been consumed with his latest project. He should have ordered something over the internet days ago. Now it was too late. Even overnight shipping probably wouldn't make it to this remote ranch in time.

"Yeah," the girls chorused.

Shaking her head, Brittany smiled at him. "I tried to get them to wait, but they insisted on giving them to you today."

He smiled back, and for the first time in years, he was thinking about buying a Valentine for someone other than a family member.

"Open mine first." Rose pointed to the envelope covered in pink-and-red squiggly lines.

"Is it your turn?" Parker hoped this wouldn't be the time that they got in an argument about turns.

Rose nodded her head vigorously and Jasmine didn't object, so everything was good. He opened the card and read the little verse.

You make me glad
Because you are the best dad
In the whole wide world.
I love you.
Rose

Parker swallowed hard as he closed the card. Finally, gaining his composure, he looked at Rose. "Thank you. That was a super card."

"Now read mine." Jasmine jumped up from her seat and pushed her card at him.

He patted her on the head, then opened the second card and prepared himself for another emotional little verse.

God gave me the best daddy.
He gave me you.
Happy Valentine's Day.
I love you.
Jasmine

Parker blinked back the moisture in his eyes and swallowed that reoccurring lump. "Thank you. You made a super card, as well."

"I love you, Daddy." Both girls hugged Parker.

"And I love you." He held them close. As the group hug ended, he looked over at Delia. "It's your turn, and while you open your cards, I'll dish up the lasagna before it gets cold."

While Delia read her cards and exclaimed over them, Parker served everyone. He ventured a glance in Brittany's direction and tried to smile. He had some Valentine's shopping to do, but how was he going to do it? Could he get Christine or Derek or one of the hired hands to get something in Stockton? That would be pretty lame—letting someone else pick out Valentine gifts for his girls. He would have to go to Stockton himself. How was he going to handle that?

As Parker enjoyed his meal and the laughter and love that surrounded him, he wondered why he cut himself off from this enjoyable time. He looked at Brittany again. Even though he rationalized that work had kept him from joining the girls for supper, he knew he'd let his fear of getting too close to her keep him away. He had to cast his fear aside for the sake of his little girls. They needed him here. If he was going to live up to those verses, he had to put them first.

The words his girls had written floated around in his mind, especially Jasmine's. Had God given him these girls? He hadn't seen God in any of the circumstances surrounding his daughters' birth or subsequent adoption, but maybe he'd been wrong. He knew how much they'd brought to his life. Had he been looking on the gloomy side of things for too long? Maybe God was smiling down on him after all.

Chapter Eight

Mounds of dirty snow framed every street corner in Stockton. Parker drove his pickup down the main drag until he spied an empty parking place. Releasing a harsh breath, he pulled into the diagonal space in front of the local pharmacy that also sold numerous gift items. He hoped he would find Valentine's presents without encountering too many people he knew.

The whole weekend had come and gone before Parker got up the nerve to make this trip. He usually went to Billings to shop, but with his looming project deadline, he didn't have the time. Stockton was his only choice.

Parker gripped the steering wheel and stared at the brick building. Snow still clung to the faded blue awning that shaded the windows. Signs advertising a plethora of goods obscured the view of the store's interior. Were other customers inside—people he didn't want to meet? He got out of his vehicle and hoped that on a Monday he would find fewer shoppers in town.

The bell over the door jangled as Parker let the door close behind him. That sound had always been a signal of good times when he and his friends had come here to the old soda fountain that no longer existed. Like so many other things in his life the jingling no longer brought him joy. He lowered his gaze, hoping the noise didn't draw attention to him.

The store looked void of customers, but Parker glanced around to make sure. A young female clerk whom he didn't recognize stood at the checkout counter and pretended to look busy. At the back the pharmacist and a pharmacy tech worked side by side. Thankfully, these people, who knew him, didn't look in his direction.

Parker grabbed a shopping cart and pushed it toward the gift section on the left side of the store. Boxes of Valentine's candy sat in a display at the front of one aisle. Red, white and pink stuffed animals of every description filled a nearby shelf. He wanted to buy something simple but meaningful for Rose, Jasmine, Delia and Brittany. He rubbed the back of his neck and wished he had a clue as to what that could be.

As he perused the aisle with the toys and games, the jangling bell drew his attention to the door. His heart jumped into his throat when he saw Linda Crawford, the mother of one of his former students. She'd been one of the people who had spoken out against him. Folks like her were part of the reason he'd decided not to try to regain his teaching position.

Would she see him? Parker stepped back, pressing his back against the nearby shelf. The woman marched to the back and appeared to be waiting at the pharmacy counter for a prescription. He heard muffled conversation and some laughter. Then she left the store, the bell's sound signaling her departure.

Relief raced through his mind, and he released the breath he'd been holding. Just when he thought it was safe to resurface from behind the shelf along the far aisle, Linda reentered the store. As the bell pealed again, their eyes met. She immediately looked away and hurried toward the pharmacy. Parker didn't miss the surprise and anxiety in her expression. Seconds later, head down, the woman scurried from the store.

Obviously nothing had changed. People still thought he was guilty.

Parker shook his head as he realized that his skulking around hadn't kept him from being detected. He was guilty of nothing and had as much right to be here as Linda Crawford did. He'd like to think he wasn't a coward, but maybe his efforts to avoid people in Stockton told a different story.

Brittany's argument that he shouldn't keep Rose and Jasmine isolated on the ranch had preyed on his thoughts ever since they'd had their disagreement on the subject. Didn't Linda's behavior show that he was right? So why wasn't he so sure anymore?

Shaking the troubling thoughts away, Parker resumed his search for gifts. He wasn't going to worry about Linda or what she might think about him. He had the truth on his side, whether anyone believed him or not.

While Parker searched the collectibles case that sat near the end of the aisle, he noticed a figurine of a little girl pushing a wheelbarrow with a puppy riding in it. Perfect for Brittany's collection of dogs. He stared at the figurine and realized that someone would have to open the case. That meant making the request—not something he wanted to do, but it had to be done.

Parker strode to the checkout counter and looked at the young woman behind the register. "I'd like to purchase something from the collectibles case."

Despite her smile, she looked annoyed. "I'll have to get a key from the manager."

"Fine. I'll wait in the gift aisle."

Parker walked back to the case as the young woman strolled to the pharmacy counter. While he waited, he picked out a couple of games and books for Rose and Jasmine. The books reminded him of Brittany's request to let the girls go to the library. Maybe she was right.

The sound of footsteps made Parker look toward the end of the aisle. Scott Barnes, the owner of the pharmacy, came around the corner as the young woman returned to the checkout register. Scott had stood on the sidelines when Parker had been falsely accused. Even though Scott had been a family friend, he'd been afraid to speak in Parker's defense for fear of alienating his customers.

When Scott met Parker's gaze, the owner's mouth tightened, and he quickly focused his attention on opening the case. Parker was almost sure the man wished he could turn and go the other way. Maybe he was regretting not handing the key over to the checkout girl.

An unexpected bravado prompted Parker to speak just to see how his brother's former friend would act. "Hello, Scott."

"Hello, Parker. What can I get for you?"

Parker silently pointed toward the figurine.

After Scott retrieved it, they stared at each other until the older man broke eye contact. He fidgeted, shifting his weight from one foot to the other. Parker took in the pharmacy owner's countenance and feared that he might refuse to sell the item.

Scott abruptly turned away. "I'll get the box for this."

While Parker waited, he looked for a gift for Delia, but he didn't see anything suitable. That meant making a trip to the yarn store where he was sure to find something for her. Would he receive the same reception in that store as he had here?

"I took the box up to Megan at the checkout counter. She'll ring everything up for you." Scott nearly sprinted back to the pharmacy as if standing there might contaminate him.

Parker paid for his purchases, then headed to the yarn store. A woman he didn't know helped him pick out a knitting bag for Delia. His heart a little lighter, he made his last stop at the florist shop to pick up the order he'd placed over the phone. The woman who took his order hadn't sounded familiar. Could he possibly avoid seeing someone he knew here, too?

His wish faded as he entered the florist shop. Mary Setran, the owner, stood behind the counter. "Hello, Parker. Your order's right here."

Parker nodded. "Thanks for getting them ready on short notice."

"You're lucky we ordered a lot of stuff in anticipation of Valentine's Day. This is a busy time for us." Although Mary seemed friendly, she didn't look him directly in the eye.

She acted in much the same way Scott had. They seemed to want to keep him at a distance. Parker couldn't help noticing the inquisitive way she looked at him. Was she wondering who the corsages were for? Parker wasn't going to satisfy her curiosity.

Driving back to the ranch, Parker let the events of the morning play through his mind. He wondered whether his presence in town would be the subject of the latest gossip. After all this time, was he paranoid to have such thoughts? Maybe not, considering the way Scott, Linda and Mary had reacted to his presence. Even though people had shunned him, much as he'd expected, he was glad he'd made the trip. He'd stepped out of his comfort zone and survived.

A knock sounded on Brittany's front door. She stood back while Rose and Jasmine answered it. As Parker and Delia stepped inside, a whoosh of cold air rustled the red, white and pink streamers draping the schoolroom. Parker carried a large bag that he set by the door as he shrugged out of his tan suede coat, then helped Delia with hers.

While Brittany put the coats away, she couldn't help thinking about how handsome Parker looked in his white dress shirt and red tie. She'd never seen him in anything other than jeans, sweaters or sweatshirts and some kind of boots. The fact that he'd taken special care to dress up for the girls' party touched her deep inside. Clearly, he was willing to make an effort to please his daughters, but she still wished he would change his mind about letting the girls go into Stockton.

At least, the prospect of this Valentine's party had garnered Rose's enthusiasm, and her uncooperative attitude had mostly abated. Brittany could only hope this new behavior would last. The sweet Valentines the girls had made her reinforced that hopefulness. Rose's acceptance lightened Brittany's heart.

Rose and Jasmine escorted their guests into the schoolroom. Brittany stood in the doorway so she could observe Parker's reaction.

"Wow! You girls have done a fantastic job decorating." He set the big bag by the table where Delia's white tea service sat as an accent on the red tablecloth.

Rose pointed to the table. "See the place cards we made so you'd know where to sit?"

"I do. I like the hearts you put on them." Parker gave one of Rose's braids a gentle tug, then pulled out a chair for Delia.

Jasmine pointed to the chair next to Parker's. "We put Brittany next to you. Now you can sit down, so we can serve you."

"I will, but first I need to get something." Parker pulled four boxes out of the bag. He handed one to each of the girls, then to Delia and Brittany.

"What's in it?" Rose asked.

"Open it." Parker helped her loosen the flap, then did the same for Jasmine.

Still standing in the background, Brittany took in the exchange between Parker and his daughters. Did he wonder about the seating arrangement? Brittany wasn't sure what to make of it, but she guessed that two little girls were trying their hand at matchmaking. Brittany continued to hold her box as Rose and Jasmine lifted the lids on theirs and peeked inside.

"Oh, pretty flowers." Rose held hers up. "What do I do with them?"

Parker sat down on the nearby folding chair and motioned for the girls to come to him. "They're corsages, and you pin them on your jumper."

"Pin mine on first." Jasmine held out her corsage to Parker.

He looked back and forth between the girls. "So it's Jas's turn?"

"Yes." Jasmine stepped in front of Rose.

"You girls look very pretty in your red jumpers." Parker didn't hesitate as he pinned the corsage consisting of a rose surrounded by jasmine on his daughter. "When did you get them?"

"Brittany gave them to us." Rose patted the front of the jumper. "Do you like the heart? You see the little flowers inside it? I have pink ones, and Jas has yellow ones."

"They're very nice." As Parker pinned on Rose's corsage, he looked toward Brittany. Questions radiated from his eyes.

What was he thinking? He had no idea she'd spent the weekend sewing the little jumpers. She'd only been here three weekends, but she hated them, even though they were her days off. She didn't know what to do with her time other than attend church on Sunday morning. The first weekend she'd gone to Heather's going-away party in Billings, but she had no intention of making the hour-plus drive back and forth to Billings to hang out with friends.

The second weekend the three hired hands had invited her to go into Stockton with them. When she learned that they intended to spend the evening in one of Stockton's bars, she declined the invitation. That wasn't her idea of fun. So she'd spent the weekend alone catching up on her reading and searching the internet for jobs. Making the little jumpers had helped pass the time.

"Thanks for getting them for the girls." Parker's voice made Brittany jump.

She smiled, hoping he didn't realize that she'd been wool-gathering instead of paying attention to what was going on in the room. "You're welcome. I enjoyed making them."

"You made them? I'm impressed."

Still holding the box containing her corsage, Brittany shrugged. "It was nothing. I have my grandma's old porta-ble sewing machine. It comes in handy sometimes."

"I would say so." Parker held out one hand. "Would you like me to pin on your corsage?"

"Sure. Looks like you're quite an expert."

As soon as Parker started to pin it on, Brittany realized her mistake in letting him do it. He was standing way too close, and every nerve in her body sensed his nearness. She hoped he couldn't hear the pounding of her heart because it sounded very loud in her own ears. The promises she'd made not to let this man impact her heart went right up the chimney, along with the smoke coming from the crackling fire.

Parker stepped back. "It looks good on your red sweater."

Brittany slowly released the breath that she didn't realize she'd been holding until that moment. "Thanks."

"Glad I could help."

Brittany quickly turned toward the girls, not wanting to read anything into the compliment or the corsage. But the corsage really was lovely. The roses and jasmine made it even more special.

Trying to clear her mind of crazy thoughts about Parker, she busied herself helping the girls get everything ready for their special lunch. They brought in the trays of raw vegeta-bles, sandwiches and cookies from the kitchen and set them on the little table Brittany had set up as a sideboard. Then Rose and Jasmine carefully poured tea for everyone.

After everyone was seated, Jasmine said a prayer. Then Rose popped up from her chair and brought the tray of vegetables to the table while Jasmine followed with the sandwiches.

"Daddy, the peanut-butter-and-jelly ones are for you." Jasmine pointed to the little squares of bread that oozed peanut butter from the sides.

Parker picked one up and placed it on his plate. "Is it okay if I try one of the other sandwiches, too?"

Rose picked up a peanut-butter-and-jelly sandwich for herself. "Sure, but you gotta eat vegetables because they're good for you."

"Okay, but I want some of those cookies." Parker peered over at the table where the tray of cookies sat.

Rose scrunched up her little face. "You have to eat your other stuff first."

Brittany tried her best to keep a straight face as she met Parker's gaze. He was also having a hard time trying not to smile. She had to remind herself that she was the nanny and nothing more. She didn't want there to be anything more—really, she didn't, especially because Parker couldn't let go of the past.

After everyone finished the main course, Brittany looked over at Rose and Jasmine. "Are you girls ready to serve the cookies and more tea?"

"Yeah." They both hopped up.

"Excuse me. I have to get something." Brittany hopped up, too. When she reached the kitchen, she leaned against the counter and took a deep breath in order to regain her equilibrium.

"Hey, there you are." Parker appeared in the doorway. "Is there something I can help you with?"

Brittany swallowed hard. "No. No, I came in here to get these little gifts for Rose and Jasmine, and I've got a little something for you and Delia."

He stepped closer. "You've already done enough."

"It's nothing." She scampered to the other side of the kitchen, grabbed the gifts from the counter and practically ran into the other room. He was probably going to think she was acting weird. Well, he would be right. She was.

Delia leaned over and patted Brittany's arm. "This has been lovely. I'm going to have to use my tea set more often."

"Any time you want to share tea with someone, call me."

Delia clasped her hands together. "That gives me an excellent idea. We can have tea every afternoon after you and the girls are done with your lessons." Delia turned to Rose and Jasmine. "How does that sound?"

Rose scrunched up her face in her usual fashion. "Can we have hot chocolate sometimes?"

"Absolutely."

Jasmine waved a cookie in the air. "And cookies, too."

The conversation with Delia had calmed Brittany's nerves and helped her regain her composure. She even managed to look Parker's way without letting his grin interfere with her thought processes. "Okay, everyone. Rose and Jasmine have some gifts for you."

The girls raced to a shelf in the corner of the room and picked up several little red-and-white gift bags. They gave them to Parker and Delia.

"Open them." Rose wiggled as she clapped her hands. "Jas and I made them together."

Parker smiled and gestured toward the older woman. "Delia should go first."

Delia held up the heart-shaped refrigerator magnet with a picture of Rose and Jasmine in the center and two colorful bookmarks, then gave Rose and Jasmine a hug. "Thank you, girls. These are perfect."

Rose turned to Parker. "Daddy, it's your turn."

"Hurry. You'll like it lots." Jasmine wiggled as much as Rose.

Parker opened up his bag and brought out cylinders of different heights covered in brown leather with little metallic horseshoes circling the top of each one. "Thank you. These are great pen-and-pencil holders and will look fantastic on my desk."

Rose tapped Parker's arm. "There's one more thing in your bag."

Parker pulled out something wrapped in tissue paper. "What could it be?"

"I know. I know." Rose jumped up and down while Parker unwrapped it. "More stuff for your desk."

"Something to hold my memo pad. Exactly what I needed." He reached over and pulled them into a big hug. "Thanks again."

"You're welcome." Rose leaned closer and whispered something in Parker's ear.

He pointed to the bag he'd brought with him. "It's in there."

Expecting the gift to be for Delia, Brittany put a hand over her heart when Rose and Jasmine approached her with the box wrapped in red foil paper with a bag of chocolate hearts intertwined in the ribbon tied around it. "For me?"

Both girls nodded. They stood over her as eager to see it as she was. Trying not to tear the beautiful paper, she carefully pulled the tape off.

Rose waved her hands up and down. "Brittany, hurry. You're opening it too slow."

Jasmine poked her little face up toward Brittany. "The gift

is from all of us—Daddy, Delia, me and Rose. Daddy said you'd like it lots cuz—"

"Jas, don't tell so she'll be surprised." Rose shook her head.

Inside the foil paper was a box that was taped shut. Brittany fumbled to loosen the tape. When she finally opened the box, another one was inside. She lifted it out and looked around the room. "Whoever wrapped this is making me work for my gift."

"Delia wrapped it, but Daddy told her how." Rose beamed as she imparted the information.

Brittany glanced over at Parker who was grinning. Her stomach did one of those nosedives, and she knew it wasn't from anything she'd eaten. When she finally got the second box open and saw the figurine of the little girl pushing a wheelbarrow with a puppy in it, she fought back tears. She didn't want to get all blubbery, but she wasn't sure she could speak. Instead, she gathered Rose and Jasmine in her arms and held them until she got her emotions under control.

When she ended the hug, she looked at the group gathered around her. "Thank you so much. It will be a wonderful addition to my collection."

Rose eyed Brittany. "Give Daddy and Delia a hug, too."

Taking a deep breath, Brittany stood. She hoped the little girls weren't counting too much on romance blossoming between their dad and her. The temptation to let it happen came with every smile and every kind word he gave her. She couldn't succumb if she knew what was good for her. But to please the girls she hugged Parker as quickly as she could, then hugged the older woman.

Brittany sat in her chair while the others opened more gifts, including the coaster set with pictures of the girls that Brittany gave Parker. After they'd opened all the gifts, the girls started the cleanup. Brittany went to put the figurine in the hutch with the rest of her collection. Even though the gift was from all of them, Parker had to have been the one to purchase it. She was afraid that every time she looked at it, she would lose a little more ground in her fight to resist her attraction to him.

As she closed the doors to the hutch, she heard footsteps and turned around. Her heart caught in her throat as Parker approached.

"You did a wonderful job with the party."

"Thanks."

"Delia and I are going to head back to the big house unless you need help cleaning up."

Brittany shook her head. "The girls and I will do it. That's part of learning to give a party. After the guests leave, you have to clean up. And I know you have to get back to work."

He fingered the brim of his cowboy hat as he smiled wryly. "Thanks for saving me on this Valentine's thing. I was tied up in the project I'm working on, and I forgot about it until you brought it to my attention."

"No problem."

"You don't know how thrilled Rose and Jasmine were about this party. That's all they talked about after they gave Delia and me the invitations."

Brittany smiled. "Thanks again for the figurine. I love it."

"You're welcome. I thought of you the moment I saw it in the store in Stockton."

"You went to Stockton?" *And he'd thought of her.*

He gave her a lopsided grin. "Yeah. It was too late to do internet shopping, so I had to make that trip. Well, I'd better get going."

She tried not to dwell on the fact that he'd gone to Stockton. She wondered how that went, but she didn't dare ask. "Bye."

As Brittany watched Parker leave, she steeled herself

against the tender feelings for him that crept into her heart. She couldn't ignore Parker's involvement in his own projects that made him forget a special day in the lives of the people he cared about. Hints of Max. She couldn't let herself be interested in another man like that, and she couldn't fall in love with a man who wouldn't let go of the hurts from the past. Parker was both of those.

Chapter Nine

Another lonely Saturday loomed ahead of Brittany as she stood in the living room and stared out the window at the big snowflakes falling lazily to the ground. The house was clean. Her lesson plans for the following week were complete. Now what could she do? This didn't look like the kind of snow that would drift, but she couldn't chance driving anywhere with her less-than-reliable car. Sometimes this job seemed like a prison.

The initial rocky start that Brittany had encountered with her charges, especially Rose, had subsided since the Valentine's party. But Brittany still didn't like the isolation for her or the twins. She still hadn't convinced Parker to let his girls go into Stockton. She often wondered what had happened on his trip to town that seemed to make him more determined than ever to keep his children away from the place.

Brittany had forged a friendship with Delia and started taking knitting lessons from her. Brittany not only enjoyed learning how to knit, but she loved hearing Delia talk about the days when Parker was a little boy and his parents ran the ranch. Brittany wished she'd known him before all the trouble. Every once in a while, she thought she might have caught a glimpse of the man Parker used to be. Would that man ever emerge for good?

While she stared out the window, she thought she saw something coming toward her, but the falling snow obscured her vision. She blinked. Yes, there was definitely something moving out there. Then she heard bells. She blinked again. Today wasn't Christmas, and she wasn't seeing reindeer, but a horse-drawn sleigh appeared in front of her house.

The black two-seater sleigh stopped, and Rose and Jasmine tumbled out of the back seat. Dressed in their ski clothes and boots, they trudged to her front door. When she opened it, they were all smiles.

"Brittany, you have to ride in the sleigh with us." Rose pointed behind her.

Brittany looked up just in time to see Parker approaching. "Interested in taking a ride?"

"I'll have to change." Brittany pulled out the sides of her sweatpants. She hated for Parker to see her in the baggy sweat suit and messy hair, but what did it matter? She was trying not to impress him, right?

Parker half smiled. "We'll give you five minutes. I would've called, but the girls wanted to surprise you."

"Do you want to come in?"

Parker shook his head. "We'd get snow all over your house."

"Okay, I'll be back in a few minutes." Brittany closed her door and sprinted to the bedroom to get ready. In record time, she stepped onto her front porch.

Seated in the back of the sleigh, Rose and Jasmine let out a loud cheer.

"Where do you want me?" Brittany pulled her stocking cap down so that it covered her ears and the results of a bad hair day. She stared at the sleigh.

Parker patted the front seat. "Right up here with me."

"Okay." This arrangement was going to be another test of her resistance to the man who had captured her interest, despite the way he cloistered himself on this ranch.

After Parker got into the sleigh, he turned and held out a gloved hand to her. She took it, and he pulled her up beside him. "You okay?"

Brittany nodded, unable to speak. Did he realize that his nearness had her discombobulated? He obviously wasn't affected by their close proximity. To him, she was only the nanny, and he was the boss, indulging his children's wish to take a sleigh ride.

"Good." He handed her a thick fleece blanket. "You can wrap this around yourself."

"Thanks." She threw it over her shoulders like a shawl.

Parker unfolded another blanket. "We'll share this one across our laps and over our legs."

"Sure." What was he going to think when all she could give were one-word responses?

Parker grabbed the reins, then turned to look at Rose and Jasmine. "We're ready to go."

The little girls clapped.

After he slapped the reins and made a clicking sound, the horse responded with a plodding gait. The bells jangled as they pulled away from her house. Brittany snuggled down in her blanket and tried to relax and enjoy the scenery. The sleigh moved down the snow-packed lane, snowflakes dancing around them.

"How are you girls doing back there?" Parker turned his head toward them.

"Good." Rose giggled. "Daddy, you and Brittany are getting covered in snow."

Parker looked at her. Smiling, he reached over and brushed snow from her knit cap. "You're beginning to look like a snowman, or should I say snowwoman?"

Parker's touch drew Brittany's attention. Their eyes met, and she couldn't look away. What emotions did she see there? Was he looking at her as a woman and not the nanny?

The girls laughed, ending the moment.

"Who's that laughing back there?" Parker chuckled.

"Daddy, you know who's back here." Rose giggled again.

"Make the sleigh go faster," Jasmine shouted.

"Sorry, Jas, but old Dusty here only goes one speed. Slow."

"I kind of like slow. You can see the scenery better." Brittany took in the pristine beauty of the landscape. Fence posts sported little piles of snow that looked like hats. The branches of the pine and cedar trees bowed under the weight of the heavy coating.

The newly fallen snow brought splendor to the ranch's landscape. She understood why Parker loved living here— how it brought him a sense of peace and helped him to forget the turmoil of life. But the beauty came from God, and He was the real peacegiver. If only Parker would acknowledge that.

Adjusting the blanket that hung over their legs, Parker looked her way. "You warm enough?"

Brittany nodded. She'd finally gotten used to his presence while he wasn't paying attention to her. Now her heart pranced in rhythm with the sleigh bells.

"How far are we going?" Rose asked.

Parker glanced back. "How far do you want to go?"

"Will you take us by the baby cows?"

"Okay, we'll take a run by the pasture where the calves are, then head back so you can make a snowman."

"Yay!" A cheerful response sounded from the backseat.

As they approached the nearby pasture, Brittany watched the cows and calves huddled together while the snow covered their coats like powdered sugar. She marveled at how the cattle withstood the cold. She turned to Parker. "How do they stay warm?"

"Cattle are amazing animals. The feed they eat keeps them warm, and they eat a lot when it's cold. The guys who run the ranch make sure the animals have plenty to eat and drink when there's a snowstorm."

"What about in a blizzard when people can't get out?"

"There's lots of preparation beforehand. And this time of year is calving season. We usually hire a couple of extra guys to help out." Parker pulled the sleigh to a stop next to the pasture fence. Rose and Jasmine leaned over the side of the sleigh.

Jasmine pointed toward the group of cattle. "Brittany, do you see the babies?"

Brittany looked back at the girls. "Yes, I see them. Aren't they cute?"

"Last year we got to see one born," Rose said.

"You did?" Brittany had never seen an animal of any kind born. She wondered about letting little kids witness a birth. "What did you think?"

Rose wrinkled her nose. "Some of it was icky."

Brittany had a hard time not chuckling at Rose's pronouncement.

"Okay, we've had enough calf gazing for one day. We'll head back home." Parker slapped the reins, and Dusty trudged forward.

With the sleigh bells ringing in her ears, Brittany glanced over at Parker. "Little girls who grow up on ranches learn about the birds and bees early, don't they?"

Parker smiled. "They do. Did you enjoy the ride?"

Brittany nodded. "Thanks for including me."

As they neared Brittany's house, Rose popped up from the backseat. "Remember we're going to make a snowman."

"Yes, I remember. I'm going to drop you girls off at Brittany's. You can work on your snowman while I take Dusty back to the horse barn and put the sleigh away."

After Parker stopped, he helped Brittany down. While he lifted Rose and Jasmine out, Brittany couldn't help wondering whether his question meant he wanted to know whether she'd enjoyed being with him. She had to add this thought to all the other zany thoughts that had blustered through her mind today. Maybe after he left, she'd be able to think rationally again.

His daughters' high-pitched giggles mingled with Brittany's laughter while they worked on the snowman. Even from a distance, Parker could see that they'd made a lot of progress since he'd left. Pulling a toboggan behind him, Parker drew closer. The sound of their happiness warmed him all the way through. Brittany had definitely been the best choice to take care of his girls, even if she did try to convince him to let her bring the twins into Stockton. Why couldn't she understand that the only way for him to keep his daughters happy and safe was to keep them away from the people who would never stop judging him?

As the snow continued to fall, everything in sight was blanketed in the frosty whiteness. Everything looked pure and clean. The title of an old hymn flitted through his mind. "Whiter Than Snow."

Was God working on him again? Parker knew the girls were. They asked him almost every week whether they could go to church with Brittany and Delia. So far he'd come up with enough reasons to say no, but he was running out of excuses.

"Daddy, come see how big our snowman is." Rose's request brought his troubling thoughts to an end.

"I see. You're almost finished. Does your snowman have a name?"

"Max." Rose patted some more snow around the snowman's middle. "We named him after Brittany's friend."

"Max is nice. We talked to him on the phone." Jasmine looked up at Brittany. "He's going to show us his lab, isn't he?"

Brittany nodded. "That's what he promised he'd do."

Parker frowned, his gut in a knot. Max. Did Brittany still have feelings for him even though she'd been the one to break off the relationship? Did he dare ask what was going on? Sure. He ought to know what his daughters were doing.

He stared at Brittany and his stomach twisted. "Max, as in Max the former boyfriend? Is it still *former?*"

She nodded. "We're still friends, but nothing else. He called to find out how I was doing, and we got to talking."

"Why were Jasmine and Rose talking to him?" *Just friends. Yeah, sure.* Parker suspected that Max wasn't thinking about being just friends. Was the guy trying to use his daughters to get back with Brittany? Parker wanted to make Brittany forget about Max. The jealous thoughts mounted in Parker's mind like a snowdrift, and he couldn't get rid of them.

Brittany chuckled. "He called one afternoon while the girls and I were playing a game. You know Rose. She had to talk to him, too."

"Yeah, Daddy. He's funny. He can talk like Donald Duck." Rose continued to work on the snowman, not having a clue that her father was trying to tamp down a mountain of jealousy.

"So he's an entertainer, too?" Parker eyed Brittany.

"Not exactly. He just likes kids. Now the girls ask me every other day when they'll get to see Max's lab." Rolling her eyes, Brittany laughed again. "I thought we'd make a field trip of it. You want to go, too?"

"I could." Parker felt silly now. She was inviting him

along. What did that tell him? He cautioned himself about reading anything into the invitation. "What kind of lab are you talking about?"

"He works as an intern in a cancer-research lab. He'll finish his graduate studies at the end of this semester."

"Sounds interesting." Parker didn't want to talk about Max anymore. He hoped the toboggan he'd discovered would steer the conversation in a completely different direction. He looked over at Rose and Jasmine who were putting the finishing touches on their snowman. "Hey, look what I found when I put the sleigh away."

Rose raced over. "What is it?"

"It's called a toboggan, and you ride it." Parker picked up the rope he'd dropped in the snow. "Get on, and I'll give you a ride over to the hill by our house."

Rose and Jasmine piled onto the toboggan. "Let's go."

"We're on our way." He put the rope over his shoulder and pulled. Brittany walked quietly beside him, and he had an unexpected feeling of contentment with her by his side. He turned and looked at Rose and Jasmine. They waved at him.

"Faster. Go faster," Jasmine yelled.

"Jas, you have a fascination with going fast today."

"Faster is more fun."

"When we get to the house, we'll see how you like going down the hill." Parker turned around and picked up his pace. The toboggan glided along behind him. Thankfully, the slight downhill grade was his friend.

"Daddy, that's good."

Parker felt a little silly trying to impress two little girls and one petite woman, but he wanted to be as much fun as Max. Parker couldn't stop himself from competing with a man who wasn't even here.

When Parker finally reached his house, he slowed his pace and brought the toboggan to a stop at the top of the knoll overlooking snow-covered pastureland. Low-hanging clouds and falling snow obscured the view of the mountains in the distance.

He looked at his passengers. "Now the real fun begins."

While the girls scrambled off the toboggan, Brittany walked toward him. "So what's on your agenda now?"

Making you see me as more than your boss or Rose and Jasmine's dad. The answer popped into his head, and he realized it was true. He couldn't deny his feelings for her anymore. But was there any chance of her returning them? He'd have to wait and see.

Before he managed to give Brittany an answer, Jasmine was jumping up and down beside him. "Will you take us down the hill on the sled?"

"That's the plan."

"I get to go first." Rose raced back to the toboggan and claimed her spot.

Parker wondered whether there was going to be an argument over who got to go first because he definitely knew it was Jasmine's turn. "Is it your turn?"

Rose pressed her lips together as if she didn't want to admit that it wasn't her turn. Shaking her head she got off the toboggan. She stuck out her lower lip, then looked up at him. "It's Jas's turn, but can I go next?"

Brittany gazed at him and put a hand on one of his arms. When she touched him, he thought the snow under his boots might melt. "Do you have other sleds, so we can all go at the same time?"

For a moment he didn't speak in an effort to gather his scattered thoughts. He took a deep breath. "Yeah, but they're the kind with runners, and they won't do well in this deep snow. They'll get stuck."

Brittany stepped away and put an arm around Rose's shoulders. "I'll keep you company while Jasmine goes with your dad. It'll be your turn in no time. And while they're sledding, you and I can make snow angels. Do you know how to do that?"

Rose's expression brightened. "Yeah. I can make a really good one."

Jasmine got on the toboggan, then turned to Parker. "Hurry, Daddy, so I can make a snow angel, too."

Parker smiled to himself as he gave the toboggan a push and hopped on. He was playing second fiddle to Brittany, but he didn't mind.

When Parker and Jasmine came to the bottom, the sled slowed and finally stopped. He jumped up and looked at his daughter. "Stay there, and I'll pull you back up."

As Parker trudged up the hill, he noticed that the snow had finally stopped falling. He would have to do a little shoveling when they finished sledding. Something told him that he was going to have a few sore muscles tomorrow. When he reached the top, Brittany and Rose were waiting for them.

Covered in snow from head to foot after her angel making, Rose ran to him and grabbed his hand. "Come see my angel."

"You made a very good one."

"You make one, Daddy."

No way. A grown man didn't lie down in the snow and do this. But if he didn't, he'd disappoint two little girls, and his stature with the red-haired woman he was trying to impress might plummet. But was he actually going to impress her by making a snow angel, or would he just make a fool of himself?

He glanced Brittany's way. She was standing there with a little smile curving her mouth. Did she suspect that he wasn't excited about this? Probably.

Parker patted Rose's head. "First, let me take you down the hill on the toboggan, then I'll make a snow angel."

"Okay." Without an argument, Rose trotted off toward the toboggan.

Relieved, at least for the time being, Parker followed. Too soon the trip down the hill was over, and he was pulling Rose back up. The whole time he tried to figure out a way to get out of making a snow angel without displeasing his kids. He couldn't think of one.

When he stopped the sled, Rose greeted him with a look of anticipation. "Now you can make the angel."

If Brittany wasn't standing there, would he have found some excuse not to do this? Absolutely. But her look of expectation prompted him not to disappoint. *Yeah. My turn to lie down in the snow and make a fool of myself.* "Okay, where do you want me to make mine?"

Jasmine pointed to an untouched area of snow. "Right next to Brittany's."

Parker lay down on the spot and hoped he didn't look too ridiculous. He rapidly moved his legs and arms to make the impression, then hopped up.

Rose and Jasmine clapped. "Yay, Daddy."

Jasmine came over and hugged his snowy form. "I like yours best."

Parker looked down at his daughter, then at Brittany who was gazing at him, admiration in her smile. Whether he made a fool of himself or not, it was worth it just to see her smile at him that way.

As they looked at the images indenting the snow, Rose pointed. "Our snow angels look like a family. A daddy, a mommy and two kids."

Parker's stomach took a dive as if it were racing down the hill on the sled. Yeah. Like a family. Rose was putting into words what his heart knew he wanted—a family that included Brittany.

Chapter Ten

Although the snow had stopped, the sky remained gray and sunless, but Rose, Jasmine and their handsome dad had filled Brittany's life with sunshine today. Now their time together was over, and Brittany hated for the fun-filled day to end, but she could hardly invite herself to stay.

Rose and Jasmine scrambled ahead through the snow as they made their way to the front of the house. Oddly silent, Parker shuffled along beside Brittany. She knew he'd been a little embarrassed to make an angel in the snow, but he'd done it, helping to make up for how often he withdrew to his office. Today was an exception. Maybe he was making an effort to do more with his kids.

When they reached the front of the three-car garage, Parker punched in a code on the keypad at the side of one of the doors. The garage door slowly opened. He motioned to Rose and Jasmine. "Into the mudroom you go."

As the kids started to leave, Brittany waved. "Rose and Jasmine, thanks for inviting me on the sleigh ride. I'm headed home now."

Rose raced back into the driveway and grabbed Brittany's arm. "Don't go. You should stay."

Jasmine joined Rose. "Please don't go. You can have soup with us."

Brittany started to speak, but before she could get any words out, Parker interrupted. "Girls, I know you love to have Brittany around, but she does deserve her time off. She might have plans."

She didn't have plans, and she wanted to spend more time with Parker and his kids, but she wasn't sure how to respond now. Did he want her to leave? If she said yes to the girls' invitation, he would be cornered into having her stay for supper.

Knitting her eyebrows, Rose looked up at Brittany. "Do you have plans?"

Even if Parker wasn't very enthusiastic about her staying, Brittany didn't want to spend another Saturday evening alone. Rose and Jasmine wanted her to stay, so she would. Besides, Brittany hoped to talk to Parker about letting the girls go to see a play at the high school in Stockton. She doubted that he would say yes, but she had to ask anyway. Maybe sometime tonight she would get that chance. "I don't have any special plans."

"Yay!" Rose and Jasmine clapped while they jumped up and down, then hurried inside.

Parker turned to Brittany. "You know, if you don't want to stay, you don't have to. I don't want the kids to be pests."

Narrowing her gaze, Brittany decided to get to the truth. "Are you trying to get rid of me?"

Parker stared at her wide-eyed and shook his head. "I didn't want to impose on your time. I thought maybe you didn't know how to turn down my overzealous children."

Brittany smiled with relief. "I love your overzealous children. They make my life an adventure."

"Whew! That's good to know." Parker ran a hand across his brow. "Do you need to run home to change?"

"Still trying to get rid of me?"

"No, but I figured your clothes are probably as wet as mine."

Brittany pulled out the sides of her ski pants. "Actually, I'm good. I threw these on over my other clothes earlier."

"Okay. Let's go inside."

A delicious aroma greeted Brittany as she stepped into the mudroom. "Something in the kitchen smells really good."

"Delia's vegetable soup and fresh bread. It's fantastic and just the thing to warm us up after a day out in the snow."

"Sounds delicious."

"It is." Parker chucked off his boots. "I'm going to check on the girls. If you decide you need anything, I'm sure I can find something in the things my sisters leave here."

"Okay, but I'm sure I'll be fine."

After Brittany got out of her ski clothes, she moseyed into the kitchen in her stockinged feet. A stockpot sat on the stove, and slices of whole-grain bread filled a wicker basket.

"Well, I hear we have special company for supper tonight."

Brittany turned at the sound of Delia's voice. "Not special, just company."

"Oh, those little girls think you're special."

Brittany smiled. "I'm glad to hear that. I don't think Rose had that opinion when I first started the job. I didn't do anything the way Miss Jenny did it."

Delia chuckled. "We all hate change, but fortunately, kids adjust better than adults."

"Thankfully." Brittany nodded.

"And I think there's a grown-up man who lives here who also thinks you're special."

Heat crept up Brittany's cheeks. How was she supposed to respond to that? "It's nice to know that he thinks I'm a good nanny for Rose and Jasmine."

Delia picked up the lid on the stockpot and stirred its contents. After returning the lid to the pot, she turned to Brittany. She started to say something, but Rose and Jasmine came bounding into the kitchen. Dressed in velour sweatsuits, they hopped up on the barstools.

"Where's your dad?" Delia asked.

Rose shrugged. "He's still changing. He's getting cleaned up because we have company."

"Is that so?" Delia raised one eyebrow and glanced in Brittany's direction. "Did he tell you that?"

Jasmine shook her head. "We know because he likes Brittany."

Delia nodded. "You girls are very observant. I believe you're right."

"Right about what?" Parker strode into the room.

"That you like Brittany."

"I do. We all do," he said without missing a beat.

Brittany blushed at the way they were talking about her as if she weren't in the room. Pretty soon her face was going to match the red appliquéd hearts on Rose's sweatsuit. Brittany still didn't know how to read Parker. His nonchalant agreement with his daughters' assessment of his feelings made her think she'd been reading way too much into his actions. Why was her silly heart leading her down this path?

After they ate supper, Brittany played Crazy Eights with Parker and the girls, then they had their bedtime story. As she and Parker gave Rose and Jasmine their good-night hugs and kisses, Brittany couldn't help thinking about being part of this family. The thought wouldn't go away, despite her earlier sense that Parker's affection for her didn't go beyond friendship.

After turning out the light, Parker stepped into the hallway. "They ought to sleep well tonight after all of today's activities."

"Yeah, I'll probably sleep well, too." Brittany followed him down the hall and into the kitchen. "Now it's really time for me to go. I don't want to wear out my welcome."

"You can't wear out your welcome." Parker laid a hand on her shoulder. "I...I was hoping you...you don't have to leave yet."

Was he nervous about asking her to stay, not for the girls, but because this was what he wanted? What did *she* want? Her emotions were beginning to feel like a yo-yo—up one minute, down the next. She tried to put on a blasé front. "I don't have to go yet."

"Good. I don't know about you, but I'm tired of kids' movies. I'm ready for something for grown-ups." He walked over to the kitchen desk, picked up a DVD case and waved it in the air. "Would you care to join me? I know weekends are your time off, and I appreciate your coming with the girls today. They love having you around, so I understand if you'd rather go. But I'll serve you popcorn if you want to watch the movie with me."

Brittany chuckled as she wrinkled her brow. "I'm not sure whether you really want me to stay or not."

He shook his head. "I'd like you to stay, but...but this is awkward...I don't want you to stay just because I'm your boss and you think you have to."

Looking him in the eye, she took a deep breath. "I'd like to watch the movie."

"Good. Let's go downstairs, and I'll make that popcorn."

As they passed through the kitchen, Delia was emptying the dishwasher. "Are the girls tucked in for the night?"

"Yes, and Brittany and I are going to watch a movie. Do you want to join us?"

Delia waved a hand at them. "No, you two go on. I've got one of my shows recorded, and I'll do some knitting while I watch it. But thanks for inviting me."

The fact that Parker had invited Delia to join them made

Brittany think that his offer to watch a movie with her was a friendly gesture and nothing more. On the other hand, had Delia turned down the invitation in order to leave Brittany and Parker alone? Was Delia taking a page from Rose and Jasmine's book on matchmaking? Brittany tried to figure it out while she followed Parker down the stairs.

Minutes later, she settled back on one of the plush chairs in the little theater. While the opening credits of the movie rolled across the screen, Parker sat down next to her and handed her a bag of popcorn and a can of pop. In the darkness, she peered at it. Her favorite kind. He remembered.

The superhero movie kept her entertained, but her mind kept wandering to the man sitting next to her. He laughed at something humorous in the movie, and she joined in the laughter. He looked her way, and her heart thudded.

He leaned closer. "Glad you're enjoying this."

"I am."

When the movie ended, Parker stretched his arms above his head, then stood. "Great entertainment."

"Thanks for sharing your movie time with me."

"We'll have to do this more often. How about a regular Saturday-night movie just for grown-ups?"

"I'd like that." Could this invitation be considered a date? Did she want it to be? Brittany cautioned herself not to go there. A date was supposed to include going out. And she knew Parker had no interest in going into Stockton, even if he did want to date her.

"Then I'll plan on it."

For a moment as they stood there looking at each other, Brittany had a feeling that he might kiss her. But then he stepped away. Maybe she'd only imagined the look in his eyes. She took a deep breath. Her mind and heart were on overload. She should go home before she read anything more into his actions.

"Now I do really need to go."

"Let me walk you home."

"It's not necessary."

"I know it's not, but I'd feel better if I did." He motioned for her to lead the way up the stairs. "I know you only live across the way, but it's dark."

"Okay."

"I'll tell Delia that I'm walking you home. Be back in a minute."

While Parker was gone, Brittany donned her ski clothes and boots for the trek home. After Parker returned and put on his jacket and stocking cap, they left the house through the garage. The pole light that illuminated the area cast long shadows as they traipsed through the snow. Silence surrounded them in the crisp, cold air. Stars flickered in the clear skies that meant a very cold night ahead. They walked to the end of the drive without saying anything, the packed snow crunching under their boots.

"Looks like one of the guys plowed the drive and the road up to your house. That'll make it easier to get around tomorrow."

"Yeah, it will." Brittany hunched her shoulders against the biting cold and wondered whether Parker was thinking about her usual trip to Stockton for church. Maybe this would be a good time to ask him about letting Rose and Jasmine go to the play with her. "I'd like to ask you something."

"What?"

Brittany hoped the good feelings that today had produced would make him open to her request. "Would you let me take Rose and Jasmine to see a play? The high-school theater department is performing *Annie*."

Parker opened his mouth to say something, but Brittany cut him off. "I know you said you didn't want them to go into Stockton, but think how much they'd love it."

A glower dominated his expression as he shook his head. "I don't think it's a good idea."

"Parker Watson, you're a good man, and I wish somehow you could get over the past." Brittany wanted so badly to heal his wounded soul.

"That's easy for you to say. You didn't live through it."

"I know. I can't begin to relate, but I know this bitterness you carry around can't be good."

Picking up his pace, he glared at her. "Maybe so, but the people in that town still don't want anything to do with me."

Brittany shook her head. "After all this time?"

"Yes." Parker practically spit the word at her. "When I went to Stockton to shop for Valentine's Day, people couldn't even look me in the eye or, if they did, they immediately looked away. I won't have my girls subjected to that."

"Are you sure that's why they looked away? Maybe they didn't know what to say."

"Whatever the reason, you can't take them to Stockton."

Brittany's pulse pounded in her brain. Had she totally sabotaged every bit of goodwill between them? But she wasn't going to give up. "Please reconsider, at least for Rose and Jasmine. I know how much you love those little girls, and I know you want what's best for them."

He didn't say anything, just clomped ahead, his footsteps sounding angry on the crusty snow. Her heart ached. She'd never intended to upset him, but what should she have expected? The man had carried this hurt around with him for over six years. Did she think she was going to waltz into his life and make things better in a matter of a few weeks?

She wanted to make his life better, but she couldn't do it by herself. He had to cooperate. As she cast a cautious glance his way, she realized one thing. She'd forgotten to pray about this before rushing ahead with her attempt to fix his life.

When they reached her front door, he finally looked at her, but he didn't say anything. His mouth painted a grim line.

"I'm sorry I butted in where I don't belong. I wish things could be different."

"Me, too."

Her heart sinking, she fumbled to open her front door. When it swung open, she looked at Parker. The scowl hadn't disappeared. What could she say to him? Words failed.

Finally, he broke the silence. "You're home safe. Have a good night."

"Good night." How could she possibly have a good night after the way things had ended with Parker? How could such a wonderful day close so badly?

She stepped inside and leaned against the door. She stood there in the semidarkness, the only light coming from a tiny night-light plugged into the hallway outlet. A tight, cold feeling gripped her chest. If he really wished things were different, why didn't he try to change?

She shut her eyes against the pain. Crying might relieve some of the hurt, but the tears wouldn't come. She whispered into the quiet house. "Lord, please help me know how to help Parker. Please soften his heart. Help him see that You care and that he needs You."

"Tomorrow, tomorrow." Buckled into their booster seats in the back of Brittany's car, Rose and Jasmine sang the song from the play at the top of their lungs.

Brittany joined in as she drove back to the ranch and hoped that she'd still have a job tomorrow. Even though she knew that defying Parker's order might get her fired, she'd decided to take the girls to see *Annie.* Right now he was so involved in his work that she doubted he even knew they'd left the ranch.

Since last Saturday, when he'd told her that she couldn't take them to the play, he hadn't eaten a single evening meal with his children. He saw them for five minutes at bedtime when he came to kiss them good-night. At least he'd done that. His inattention to the girls in the past week had convinced her that she should take them. They needed more interaction than she could give them by herself, and he wasn't doing his part to help. They'd enjoyed the movie, and now they'd seen the play.

The trip to Stockton had concluded without any problems, but what consequences awaited her decision to disobey Parker's order? She hoped against hope that he would see that he'd been wrong—that he'd been unduly paranoid about the people there.

As Brittany drove into the garage, her cell phone rang, but she ignored it. She would deal with it later. The girls quickly unbuckled themselves and charged toward the door leading into her house. She'd already planned with Parker for the girls to have a sleepover, but had kept the first part of the evening a secret from him. Before they got there, the door swung open. Parker stood in the doorway, phone in hand and anger narrowing his gaze.

So that's who had been calling her.

"Daddy, Daddy." Rose and Jasmine greeted him with hugs.

Parker's expression softened as he hugged his girls, but anger still brewed in his eyes when he glanced at her.

Brittany swallowed hard as she approached, her stomach churning. Did she dare speak? She certainly didn't want to argue with Parker in front of Rose and Jasmine, and judging from the expression on his face there would soon be a heated discussion, if not a full-blown argument.

Rose held up the canvas bag with a picture of Annie on it. "See what Brittany bought us?"

Parker nodded, but a frown furrowed his brow as he again looked her way.

"We got more stuff, too." Rose pulled a red curly wig from the bag and tried to put it on.

Brittany watched for Parker's reaction. He appeared to be fighting a smile. A sense of relief tentatively settled around her heart. "Rose, Jasmine, let's go inside and show your souvenirs to your dad."

The girls scrambled past Parker as they raced into the house. Parker stood aside, and Brittany hurried through the door, unable to look him in the eye. Despite his almost smile, he was still angry, and she would eventually have to answer to him for her actions.

Brittany helped Rose and Jasmine put on their *Annie* wigs. Then the two girls did a little song and dance for Parker. Surely he could see how much fun the experience had been for them.

When they finished, Parker applauded. "Very good. Now it's time for you to get ready for bed."

"Do we have to?" Rose scrunched up her face.

"Yes. I came over to read you a bedtime story." Parker waved Rose and Jasmine toward the extra bedroom.

"I'll help them." Brittany started to follow the girls.

Parker gently grabbed Brittany's arm. "They can get ready by themselves, and we're going to talk."

Her heart pounding in her ears, Brittany stopped. This was it. He was going to fire her, but he couldn't do that if Rose and Jasmine were spending the night, could he? Maybe he was only going to scold her, but he couldn't yell at her with the girls in the next room.

Determined to defend herself, Brittany took a deep breath. "I know you said they couldn't go, but—"

"But you decided you knew better. You took advantage when I agreed that they could spend the night here. Even though I arrived only minutes ago, don't you think I was worried when I found you gone?" Parker's words spewed out in low tones through gritted teeth. Then he stared at her, his hands curled in fists at his side.

Brittany swallowed a big lump in her throat. "I'm sorry if you were worried, but can't you see how much fun they had? No one said anything unkind. In fact, people were very nice."

Before she could say anything else, Rose and Jasmine came bounding into the room. They each carried a book that they handed to Parker. He settled on the couch with the girls on either side of him as he read. With each word, the rigid set of his shoulders abated, but Brittany knew she hadn't seen the last of his anger.

After Parker tucked the girls into bed, Brittany left the room and Parker followed. She could almost feel the daggers of disapproval aimed at her back and feared facing him.

"Brittany, I still have some things to say."

His clipped tone didn't bode well for the conversation. Her heart in her throat, she slowly turned. "Sure."

"Your actions call into question your judgment." Despite the unhappiness in his voice, the displeasure had faded from his face.

Even though she might make matters worse, she wasn't going to let him get away with questioning her judgment. "But the results call *your* judgment into question, too. I told you no one said an unkind word to them. No one. In fact, one of the ladies from church came over and talked with them. She was extremely friendly. Then a couple of your former students said to tell you hello. Doesn't that convince you that not everyone thinks you were guilty?"

"Well, maybe they were nice to you, but I know how people react to me when I go to town."

Parker wasn't listening to reason. Things couldn't get much worse, so she might as well tell him what she thought. She pointed a finger at him. "You're the one who has lost perspective about the situation."

"You've said about enough. You—"

"You just don't want to listen to the truth."

"The truth is if it weren't for Rose and Jasmine's attachment to you and the fact that I'm tied up with this project, I'd fire you. So you have a reprieve, but one more incident like this and you're gone. Understood?"

Even though she knew the consequences of taking the girls to the play could mean losing her job, to hear Parker say it made the possibility all too real. Tears threatened at the thought, but she fought them as she nodded. She would not let him see her cry.

"Have a good night." Parker turned and left without another word.

How could she possibly have a good night? Brittany sank onto the couch and let the tears come as she asked God to forgive her for her actions. At least Parker hadn't fired her, but would she be under constant scrutiny now? Had she lost his good opinion forever? Well, she'd have to live with the consequences, but even though she was sorry she had defied Parker, she knew she'd done the right thing. The girls needed this kind of activity. He couldn't keep himself or his children isolated on this ranch forever. She'd just have to pray that he would eventually realize that, too.

Chapter Eleven

Wind whistled around every corner of the house as the blizzard swept across the ranch. Parker stood by the living-room window overlooking the backyard while blinding snow obscured everything in sight. A four-foot snowdrift sat on the deck right outside the window.

When things were going well with the ranch, he didn't think about it much. He left everything related to the cattle operation to Derek and his crew, but Parker understood what a blizzard could mean to the bottom line in an operation that, in reality, didn't make a lot of money. Income from the ranch wasn't an issue for him, but people like Derek and the other cowhands depended on this ranch for their living. Parker wanted to make sure they could still do the things they loved—riding the range and tending to the cattle. Although Parker had no interest in doing this work himself, he still wanted to see the ranch remain a working ranch as a tribute to the generations of Watsons who had raised cattle here. A bad storm could put that in jeopardy.

Maybe he should pray. The thought blew him away, as if he were out in the storm. Before supper tonight, Rose and Jasmine had prayed for the cows and their calves. Could that account for the unexpected thought?

Despite the storm, the inside of the house was cozy and warm. Although the sound of conversation and laughter buzzed around him, he felt no joy because he'd alienated Brittany. Over the past couple of weeks, he'd tried to put their disagreement behind him, but it sat in his mind like the snowdrift. Even early this morning, while Parker had helped move the cattle to sheltered areas and put out feed before the bad weather hit, thoughts of Brittany dominated his thinking. Now he only wanted to think about not losing any of the herd, but, instead, he was more worried about losing Brittany.

"You can't do anything about the storm, so you might as well come and join the fun."

Parker turned at the sound of Derek's voice. "Yeah, I know, but I can't help looking at it. I'm just glad we're all safe here."

"Thanks to your foresight in putting in a generator."

Parker nodded. "It keeps things going when the power's out."

"Christine said we're planning to play a little trivia game after we get the kids settled for the night. I plan to recruit you to answer the science questions for my team."

"But don't ask me any of that pop-culture stuff." Parker shook his head. "Did Delia show you the spare bedroom?"

"Yeah. Thanks for letting us stay here."

"No need to thank me. I'm glad we could accommodate everyone during the storm. You've got a good group of cowboys."

Derek nodded. "They know how to get the job done."

"I could see that while we were working today."

Parker had to admit that he'd enjoyed the day, even though he hadn't ridden in a long time and would probably feel it tomorrow. Today's activities made him realize that he shouldn't spend all his time cooped up in his office, away from the people who worked his ranch—or his kids or Brittany. The day the girls had insisted they should take Brittany for the sleigh ride was the last time he'd taken the opportunity to have fun. Then he'd gone and pushed Brittany away with his harsh words. Although he believed he was right, he was sorry he had spoken to her so brusquely. He hated the distance he had created between them, but he wasn't sure how to apologize.

Derek clapped Parker on the back, breaking his troubled line of thinking. "Looks like Christine's putting DJ to bed. I think Rose and Jasmine are helping, too. So I need to say good-night to my little guy. Can I count on you for that trivia game?"

"Sure. I'll go with you and make sure my girls are headed to bed, too."

When they arrived at the spare bedroom, Rose and Jasmine were reading a bedtime story to DJ. Parker watched with pride swelling his heart. He loved these little girls. He hardly ever remembered that they were adopted. They were his kids.

When they finished, Rose raced over to him. "Daddy, we got to read. Did you hear?"

"I did."

Rose tugged on his arm. "Where's Brittany? Delia asked her to do something, but she hasn't come back. We have to say good-night to Brittany."

"Girls, get your pajamas on, and I'll go find her."

"Okay." Rose and Jasmine raced down the hall to their bedroom.

When Parker stepped into the living room, Brittany was passing out bedding to the guys who were sleeping on the rollaway beds in the basement. The cowboys laughed at something Brittany said. One named Curt put an arm around her shoulders. She looked up at him and smiled.

Jealousy hit Parker like a well-placed snowball to the

chest. His breath caught in his throat. Since the confrontation over the play, Brittany had kept her distance. She went about her duties, but kept to herself on the weekends. He missed watching movies with her on a Friday or Saturday night after the girls were in bed.

Rose and Jasmine bugged him constantly about wanting to see Brittany on the weekends or about going to church with her and Delia. His daughters were beginning to wear him down with their incessant requests. His arguments against it were starting to seem pretty thin. He hated to admit that he was wrong, but the evidence mounted against him. His girls had survived, even flourished, after their trip to Stockton. They wanted to go again, and visit the library and church.

Sometimes he wanted to relent, but he didn't want to hear Brittany say, "I told you so." He wanted to please his daughters and rebuild his closeness to Brittany, but if the price was giving up his suspicion of the people in Stockton, could he handle it?

His reluctance to get over that troubled time in his life was developing into the one big thing that stood between them. Maybe he was going to have to come to grips with that before some cowboy like Curt came along and grabbed Brittany's attention, leaving Parker alone with the bitterness that still held him captive.

As Parker approached the group, he was quite happy to break up their fun. "Brittany."

She turned at the sound of his voice and smiled, much to his surprise. He wanted that smile just for himself. The jealousy was making him think crazy things. She was the kind of person people gravitated toward. People loved her because she was fun to be with. She lavished her smile on everyone around her. Even if she were in love with him, he'd never have a corner on her smile.

"Hey, we were just talking about you." She waved him over. "I was telling them about how you made a snow angel."

"Best snow angel you'll ever see." He looked over the group. Were they laughing at him?

"That's what Britt says." Curt eyed Parker. "She also tells us that you're an excellent skier. She said you helped her when she first learned to ski even after she fell out of the chairlift."

The group chuckled again, and Parker was ashamed of himself. He should've known better. Brittany was laughing at herself, not at him. She'd said nice things about him. Was she warming up to him again? He didn't know how to read her.

Parker cautioned himself not to read anything into the conversation or Curt's attention to Brittany. Being jealous was pointless. If Brittany was interested in one of the cowboys, he had no right to interfere. Parker wanted to convince himself of that, but the message wasn't making it to his heart.

Parker felt the need to say something good about Brittany. "She's actually a very competent skier."

"Yeah, as long as I stick to the easy slopes."

"Well, I have an easy slope for you to tackle right now. Rose and Jasmine want you to come in and say good-night."

"Sure." Brittany turned to the other guys. "You have everything you need?"

A chorus of yeses filled the air as Parker departed with Brittany by his side. He tried not to feel smug as he led her away from Curt.

When Parker escorted Brittany into Rose and Jasmine's bedroom, the little girls hugged Brittany as if they hadn't seen her all day.

Jasmine scurried to the bookshelf in between the beds and grabbed a book. She turned to Brittany. "Are you going to read another chapter?"

Brittany looked at him. "Is that all right?"

Parker nodded. "Must be a good book."

"It is, Daddy." Jasmine sat on the bed beside Brittany.

Rose sat on the other side. "It's about a racehorse, and he' going to run in the Kentucky Derby. We want to see if h wins. You should listen, too."

"Okay." Parker leaned against the doorjamb.

Jasmine nodded. "Old Bones is the horse's name."

Brittany began to read, and Parker let the sound of he voice wash over him. He remembered the first time she'd rea to the girls and how she'd made the story and the character come alive. Tonight was no different. She had him rooting fo the horse to win, even though he knew the outcome. Whe Old Bones won the race, the girls cheered.

After Brittany read the rest of the chapter, Parker listene to the girls' prayers. When they prayed again for the safet of the cows and their babies, Parker found himself prayin right along with them. He didn't know what was happen ing to him. He guessed that Brittany and his daughters wer making him a better man despite himself.

After the good-night hugs and kisses, Parker turned ou the light. He and Brittany quietly stepped into the hallway He wished he could apologize to her, but this wasn't the tim or the place. They needed privacy, and there was none of i in this house tonight.

While they walked in silence he wondered whether h could rid himself of the fear of being rejected again—th fear that kept him from pursuing a romantic relationship wit Brittany.

When they reached the living room where a fire crack led in the wood-burning fireplace, Derek motioned for the to come over. "Hey, we've got our trivia teams ready to go Parker, you're with me, and Brittany, you're on Curt's team."

Parker wanted to protest but forced himself to smile in

stead. Throughout the evening, he had a hard time focusing on the questions because his attention was on Brittany and Curt. The cowboy was definitely trying to impress her.

Despite the attention Brittany was getting from the other guys, Parker enjoyed listening to her trump their knowledge on the sports questions. She was a storehouse of trivia. Still, when the game finally ended, Derek's team had won.

The group said their good-nights and headed to their assigned sleeping quarters. Parker couldn't help noticing Curt's special attention to Brittany as he said good-night to her. The jealousy that he'd managed to tamp down during most of the evening resurrected itself. But he reminded himself that he had no right to interfere. Not when he still wasn't sure that after years of closing himself off, he was ready to let go of the past and be vulnerable to love again.

The following morning Parker woke up to silence—a good sign. The wind had quit blowing. He glanced at the clock on his bedside table. The bright red digital numbers read 6:50. A little stiff from the previous day's activities, he walked to the window and opened the basement blinds. A snowdrift greeted him. He wondered whether the whole house was encased in snowdrifts.

By the time Parker had put on his warmest clothes, he heard voices in the rec room. He poked his head out the door. Curt and the other guys were heading up the stairs. Parker hurried to join them.

"What do you think we'll find out there this morning?" Parker asked.

Curt turned to him. "Hopefully, we'll find cows and calves in good shape. We had two cows in the calving barn. We'll have to see if they had their calves. You going with us?"

"Yeah. You may need my help to dig out."

Parker joined the others as they cleared snowdrifts away

from the doors and used the snowblower to make a path to the horse and storage barns so he could get the tractor with the plow mounted on the front. The cowboys went out to feed and water the cattle while Parker stayed behind to plow the roads on the ranch.

After the cowboys returned, Parker joined in the laughter and backslapping that ensued when they reported that every single cow and calf had survived the storm. As they made their way into the house, Parker couldn't help thinking about the answered prayers of his little girls. Did he dare make prayer a part of his life again? If he did, he feared God would ask him also to extend the forgiveness that seemed so elusive.

The smell of bacon and cinnamon rolls permeated the air as Parker and the others walked into the kitchen. While Brittany, Delia and Christine put out a breakfast buffet, Derek and Curt reported the good news about the cattle.

Delia swatted Parker's hand as he attempted to steal a roll. "You have to wash up first. Besides, we're not quite ready."

While the group waited to eat, Derek hunkered down to talk with Rose and Jasmine. "During the storm, we had two cows have their babies. Maybe your dad will take you out to see them."

Instantly, Rose and Jasmine cornered Parker, and Rose acted as the spokesperson. "Daddy, did you hear? There are two new calves. Can we go see them?"

"After breakfast."

"Yay!" the girls chorused, then ran to tell Brittany the news.

Delia banged a spoon on a kettle, and the group quieted. "Breakfast's ready, and I think a prayer of thanks is in order for the food and for all that survived the blizzard."

Parker wondered whether Delia was expecting him to pray. He hoped not.

"Daddy, let me pray." Rose's high-pitched voice was music to Parker's ears.

"Sure, go ahead."

While his sweet little daughter thanked God for their blessings, Parker let her words settle in his heart. Although he hadn't wanted to pray, for the second time in recent days, he found himself praying along.

The last to go through the food line, Parker surveyed the room. Derek, Christine and DJ sat at the kitchen table with Delia, while everyone else was at the dining-room table.

"Daddy." Jasmine waved a hand in the air. "Over here. We saved a place for you."

Parker couldn't help smiling when he saw the empty chair in between Jasmine and Brittany. He suspected that his daughters were playing matchmaker again.

Jasmine tapped Parker on the arm. "Daddy, we prayed that all the cows and their babies would be okay. God answered our prayers."

Parker had to smile. Yes, God answered prayers—including the prayer from Brittany and his family that he feel the urge to let God back into his life. Still, Parker realized that he couldn't be totally right with God unless he did a whole lot of soul searching and faced some people he didn't want to face. Changes in his thinking seemed to be coming at him fast and furious. First, he had to make things right with Brittany.

Maybe that one hard icy spot in the middle of his heart might melt after all.

"Let me give you a ride home." Curt pointed to Brittany's suitcase near the door to the mudroom. "You can't drag that thing through the snow even if the roads are plowed."

Just as Brittany was about to reply, Parker walked into the kitchen. "Curt, what're you doing here?"

"Derek asked me to bring this by." Curt handed Parker an envelope.

"Thanks." Parker looked at it, then stuck it in his pocket before looking her way. "You ready?"

Brittany nodded. "But you don't have to give me a ride. Curt said he would."

"No need for you to go out. Britt's place is right on my way back to the bunkhouse." Curt picked up Brittany's suitcase.

"Yeah, now you'll have more time to work on your project." She glanced at Parker, who seemed displeased for some reason.

A strange look passed over Parker's face. She didn't know what to make of it. Was Parker still angry about the incident with the play? She'd been avoiding him up until the blizzard, and, from all indications, he'd been avoiding her, too. The presence of all the other people in the house had thrown them together, and it seemed they had both pretended that everything was okay. But the issue of her defiance must still be fresh on his mind.

"Fine by me." Parker shrugged, his disgruntled expression still in place.

During the short ride to her place, Brittany and Curt talked about how grateful everyone was that the cattle survived the blizzard. He carried her suitcase and set it inside her door.

"Thanks. I appreciate the ride."

"My pleasure." Curt touched the brim of his cowboy hat. "Mind if I ask a personal question?"

"Depends on how personal."

"I was thinking about asking you out, but I got the distinct impression that might displease the boss man."

Brittany didn't know how to respond. What was Curt implying? "I don't know why you'd say that."

Curt grinned. "I just thought he seemed to be staking out his territory where you were concerned."

Was that true? Did Parker have romantic feelings for her? "I don't know about that, but right now I'm not interested in anyone. Sorry."

Curt shrugged. "That's okay, but if you change your mind, let me know."

"Okay. Thanks again." Wondering whether Curt was right about Parker, she waved as he hurried back to his pickup. After closing the door, she sagged against it and shut her eyes.

Home at last.

She'd made it through two days living in close quarters with Parker. Surviving the tension between them had been difficult and exhausting. Thankfully, the other people in the house had served as a buffer. Now relief surged through her. She didn't have to pretend everything was okay between her and Parker. Surely the strain between them meant that Curt was wrong. Did she want Parker to have feelings for her?

Despite their problems, she'd seen changes in him that gave her hope. He'd come out of the office when the others had needed him, and he'd helped with the cattle. He'd joked with the cowboys, taken the girls to see the newborn calves and made everyone laugh when he'd given them a sleigh ride.

After they returned to the house, Parker had played with Rose, Jasmine and DJ. Parker made the little boy laugh and squeal with delight as they played tag around the island in the kitchen. Brittany couldn't help imagining Parker with a little boy of his own.

As Brittany closed the blinds on the front window, a shadowy figure materialized in the moonlight. Her heart jumped into her throat as the figure came toward the house. The yard light gave little clue as to the person's identity. She took a calming breath. Even though she wasn't expecting company, she shouldn't be frightened. The ranch was a safe place.

She closed her eyes and said a little prayer for safety.

When she opened them, the unknown person knocked. "Who's there?"

"Brittany, it's Parker."

"Parker?"

"Yeah, may I come in?"

Why was he here? She'd have thought he'd be happy to continue avoiding her. She opened the door. "Is something wrong?"

"Yeah." A muscle worked in his jaw as he looked at her. His Adam's apple bobbed. "I've been bullheaded. I know how much you care about Rose and Jasmine."

Brittany frowned. "I do, but what are you getting at?"

"Are you going to make me stand out here in the cold?"

"Oh, no, I'm sorry." Brittany shook her head. "You surprised me. Come in."

Parker stepped inside and closed the door, then glanced around. Why didn't he say something—explain what he meant?

She put a hand over her heart. "Please tell me why you're here."

"Um…yeah. I've changed my mind."

Brittany's pulse pounded all over her body. "About what?"

"About letting Rose and Jasmine go into Stockton."

His words didn't sink in for a second. When she finally realized what he had said, she stared at him, too stunned to speak.

With his arms crossed in front of him, he swayed from foot to foot as he met her gaze. "I know you wouldn't do anything that would hurt them. So I'm going to trust your judgment. If they want to go to Stockton, you can take them to the library, to church, wherever you think is best. And you should drive my SUV. It'll be safer than your car on the snowy roads." He put a hand on the doorknob. "That's all I have to say."

Not waiting for a response, he opened the door.

"Wait." Brittany immediately thought about Max's invitation to see the lab. When he'd called the day before the blizzard and told her he could show the girls the lab on Friday, she'd put him off. She feared even mentioning it to Parker, even though it was a trip to Billings, not Stockton.

Parker stopped, then turned but didn't say anything, just looked at her.

"Thank you."

"I should be thanking you for making me see my mistake."

"I know two little girls who are going to be very happy."

"That's all that counts." He started to go again.

"Good. Then you'll want to go with us when we go to Billings."

"For what?"

Brittany explained Max's invitation. "So you'll go, right?"

He gave her a wry smile. "Yeah."

Brittany grinned from ear to ear and resisted the urge to hug Parker. "You won't regret your decision."

He opened the door. "I hope you can forgive me for my harsh words."

Brittany nodded. "That's all behind us."

Before she could say anything else, Parker hurried away. She closed the door and leaned against it again. Only this time she didn't ache inside. Her spirit soared. Parker was entrusting his precious children and his vehicle to her care. God was already answering her prayer. He'd softened Parker's heart.

Chapter Twelve

"Are we there yet?" Rose's whine sounded over the hum of the tires on the road as Parker drove his SUV toward Billings.

Brittany turned and looked at the girls, who were strapped into their booster seats. "Only a few more miles."

"Yay! Then we get to meet Max." Jasmine clapped.

Rose joined in. "Will he talk like a duck?"

"If you ask him, I'm sure he will." Brittany smiled, hoping that seeing Max again wasn't a mistake.

Brittany glanced over at Parker as he gripped the steering wheel and stared straight ahead. What was he thinking? Was he wishing that he was home working on one of his projects instead of driving into Billings? Just the fact that he'd agreed to let the girls go and decided to go with them gave Brittany more hope that he was changing for the better.

Parker pulled into the parking lot of the research facility where Max worked. Brittany was glad Parker had come with them because she wasn't sure about how things would go with Max. Having Parker along would make Max realize this was a friendly visit and nothing more. She didn't want him to get any ideas that their relationship could be rekindled. Not that she had any reason to believe he was thinking that way, but she didn't want to take any chances. Her emotions were a jumbled mess because she couldn't figure out what was going on with Parker. She didn't need to add unwanted attention from Max to the mix.

While they waited in the lobby, Rose and Jasmine's excited chatter and Parker's quiet demeanor helped Brittany calm her anxiety. Everything would be good. She shouldn't be nervous. Max was her friend, and this was a great opportunity for the girls to see what happened in a laboratory.

Max strode through the door, and Brittany held her breath as he approached. He smiled and gave her a quick hug. "Good to see you."

"You, too. You look official in your lab coat."

He nodded. "After your tour, I have to go back to work."

Brittany turned to Parker and the girls. "I want you to meet my students and their dad. This is Rose, Jasmine and Parker Watson."

Max shook hands with Parker, then hunkered down to talk to the kids. "Good to meet you lovely ladies in person. Are you ready to see some cool stuff?"

The girls nodded, clearly enamored with Max. He did have a way with women, even if he was bad at relationships.

Rose blurted, "Will you talk like a duck?"

Standing, Max grinned. "If you're good during the tour, I'll give you the duck special when we're done."

"We'll be really good." Jasmine nodded her head and looked at Rose, who also nodded in agreement.

"Okay. Follow me." Max led them down a hallway.

Wide-eyed, Rose and Jasmine hung on every word Max said as he explained how they took samples from the patients. He showed them how the people in the lab made the slides, and he let them look through a microscope. They put on lab gloves and surgical masks just like the lab workers.

Brittany stood with Parker off to the side. He leaned closer and whispered, "I think your old boyfriend is charming my daughters."

"But he'll never hold a candle to you in their eyes." *Or in mine.* The phrase stuck in her mind. She was just glad that she hadn't uttered it out loud.

"Thanks. I was a little worried that his duck impression might tip the scales in his favor."

Brittany laughed softly. "No one will ever take your place. Believe me."

The saying applied to her, as well. Despite Parker's faults, Brittany couldn't dismiss her feelings. They clung in her heart, and nothing seemed to shake them. Were her emotions leading her down the wrong path again—letting her fall for the wrong kind of man? But he was changing, wasn't he? He'd made this trip for Rose and Jasmine. That had to be a positive sign.

She glanced at Parker, who was as engrossed as his daughters in Max's explanations. Must be the scientist in him. She should probably learn more about Parker's work. She was beginning to realize that she'd never paid much attention to Max's. Maybe that had been part of the problem in their relationship.

After the tour was over, true to his word, Max did his duck impression. The girls clapped and cheered. Then he gave them each a bag filled with plastic test tubes, other lab containers and the lab gloves and surgical masks they'd worn earlier. As they walked back to the lobby, Parker fell in step beside Max, and they began to talk. Brittany wondered what they were talking about, but she didn't want to intrude on their conversation.

When they reached the lobby, Parker shook Max's hand. "Thanks so much for giving us the tour."

"Glad to do it." Max walked over to the receptionist's desk, reached behind it, then turned to Parker. "Here's my phone number. When you have a chance give me a call and we'll talk."

"I will." Parker opened the door. "Thanks again."

As the girls sprinted toward the SUV, Brittany could hardly contain her curiosity. "What was that all about?"

Parker opened the door for Rose and Jasmine. "Nosy, aren't you?"

Brittany helped buckle the girls into their booster seats. "I am."

Parker laughed as he slid behind the wheel. "Max and I talked about possibly hiring me to write some of their reports. He's going to pass along my information to the lab's director."

"That would be nice."

"Yes, it would."

On the way home, Brittany kept thinking about the circumstances that had brought Parker and Max together. The whole thing seemed odd. She wasn't sure how she liked having her old boyfriend working with the guy she wished was her new boyfriend. Yes. With every passing day, the idea of a romantic relationship with Parker was something she wanted more and more.

After the lab visit, Parker drove toward the ranch. Puffy clouds filled the sky that sat above the fields like a giant blue canopy. The sun hung just above the mountains in the distance. Rose and Jasmine watched a movie on the built-in DVD player while Brittany read a book. The quiet interior of the car left Parker alone with his thoughts.

The day had turned out better than he'd expected. He'd come on the trip hoping Brittany wouldn't find a renewed interest in Max. When Parker realized that Brittany and Max were only friends, as she had claimed, relief had flooded his mind. He wanted to win her heart, but he needed time to straighten out his life. He wasn't sure how he was going to make things right with God and the people he used to know. Those things would have to come first before he could think about loving Brittany.

As Parker took the Stockton exit off Interstate-90, Brittany touched his arm. He glanced over at her. His pulse raced. "Did you want something?"

She nodded, her eyebrows raised. "It's close to suppertime. It would be a treat if we took the girls to eat at the Steakhouse Restaurant in Stockton."

Parker's stomach plummeted at the thought. Was this a test to see whether he was true to his word about trusting her judgment when it came to letting the girls go to Stockton? "Yeah, it probably would, but Delia is expecting us for supper."

"I'll call and see what she has planned." Brittany pulled her cell phone out of her purse.

Hoping against hope that Delia would save him from Brittany's suggestion, Parker tried not to listen to her phone conversation. His instinct was to insist they go home, but he had to show Brittany he'd meant what he said. Maybe this would be a step toward getting his life back on track.

He had to take chances that he hadn't been willing to take before now. Wasn't that why he'd admitted to her that he'd been wrong about keeping the kids away from town?

Brittany ended the call and turned to him with a grin. "Delia says she can save the meal she's fixing for tomorrow night. So we can go to the Steakhouse."

"Okay." He hoped this wasn't a mistake. Mondays weren't usually busy days at the Steakhouse, so maybe he wouldn't run into anyone he knew. *Wishful thinking.*

The full parking lot at the restaurant didn't ease Parker's mind. While Rose and Jasmine scrambled out of the backseat, he tried to tell himself that everything would be okay. He lagged behind the trio of females as they walked to the door. He wondered whether Brittany knew how much he didn't want to be here. Did she realize, despite his trepidation, that he was doing this to please her?

Rose and Jasmine jostled for position as they approached the hostess stand just inside the door. Conversation and laughter floated from the main part of the restaurant. Parker scanned the rustic interior with barn-siding walls, thick wooden tables and sturdy chairs. Nothing had changed since the last time he'd stepped foot in this place in happier times.

From this vantage point, he didn't see anyone he knew. Maybe his wish for anonymity would come true. While the hostess led them to a table near the front, he looked straight ahead. He made sure to sit so he had his back to most of the other diners, then buried his face in the menu.

Jasmine tapped his arm. "Daddy, what should we order?"

Parker smiled across the table at his girls. This was a treat for them, so he had to quit being paranoid and thinking too much of himself. "See what's on the kids' menu."

"Where's that?" Rose wrinkled her little brow.

"Right here." Parker pointed at one corner of the menu. "How about the burger and fries?"

"Mr. Watson?"

His stomach churning, Parker looked up. Tara Madsen, a tall slender blonde who had been his student years before, stood next to the table with an order pad in her hand. "Hi, Tara."

"It's good to see you. I'm your server this evening. What can I get you to drink?"

Her friendly demeanor left Parker speechless. Brittany quickly ordered for herself and the girls. Finally, he recovered and placed his order. Tara left to get their drinks.

"Daddy, how do you know that lady?" Rose scribbled on the place mat with the crayons Tara had left.

"When I taught school, she was one of my students."

Jasmine nodded her head. "I know you were a favorite teacher."

"How do you know that?" Parker gazed at his daughter.

"When we went to the play, some people told Brittany that you were their favorite teacher." Jasmine glanced at Rose.

"Yeah, Daddy, that's what they said." Rose resumed her coloring as if her statement was nothing out of the ordinary.

Parker turned to Brittany. She looked at him with an I-told-you-so expression. He acknowledged it with a nod. Had he been so wrong to hide away on his ranch? He gazed across the room. A couple he knew sat two tables over. When they saw him, they frowned and turned away. So he still had his detractors, but he wasn't going to let them ruin his evening.

When Tara returned with their drinks and began to take the rest of their order, Parker decided he had to quit hiding behind his fear of rejection. "How are Blake and your little girl?"

"I guess you didn't know. Blake was killed in an accident on the ranch where he worked five years ago."

"No, I didn't. I'm sorry." Parker grimaced. "How are you doing?"

Sadness crept into Tara's blue eyes. "Things have been tough. Besides losing Blake, Hailey's been sick, and her doctor is still trying to figure out what's wrong. People at church are praying for her."

Parker almost said he'd pray for her, too. Was God pulling on him from all directions? Brittany, his girls, the blizzard and now this? "That's good."

"Well, I'd better get your order in and tend to my other tables."

Parker took a gulp of his cola, his mind in a whirl. He'd been so focused on his own grievances that he hadn't thought to wonder what troubles others were going through, too. Why had he forgotten that the students had stood by him? Maybe because they'd had no say or little influence on the adults, who had turned against him, and he had let himself focus on the negative instead of remembering the good. They'd done their best to stand by him, but he'd turned his back on all of them.

Rose laid her crayon on the table. "Daddy, I want to pray for the sick girl."

"Me, too." Jasmine laid her crayon on the table and bowed her head. Right there in the restaurant, his little girls prayed for Hailey.

When they finished their prayer, Brittany reached over and patted the girls' hands. "That was very nice."

Parker nodded. "That's a tough situation for Tara."

Brittany turned to him. "I realize now that I know Tara's grandmother. I met her at church."

"You talked with Kate Pitman?"

Brittany nodded. "She was one of the first people who greeted me the first time I attended church. When she asked the church to pray for Tara, Kate said that Tara's afraid of losing her job because she's had to take so much time off from work for Hailey's doctor appointments. And if she loses her job, she'll lose her health insurance. It's a vicious cycle."

"That *is* tough." Parker grimaced as he tried to put himself in Tara's place.

"She's been working double shifts so she can get some of her coworkers to cover for her when she has to be off." Brittany shook her head. "That worries Kate."

As he listened to Brittany, he realized that he had so much compared to other people, and yet, he'd spent the past six years feeling sorry for himself. He was beginning to see that he hadn't been thankful for what he had. God was definitely working on him again.

When Tara brought their food, Parker noticed the dark

circles under her eyes that he hadn't seen when she'd taken their order. He wished there was something he could do to help her. All he could do was try to pray…and hope that God was listening.

After spending the day with Brittany, Parker kept thinking about how she was changing his life—making it better, making *him* better. He cared for her, but the thought of exposing himself to the chance of being hurt again worried him.

He went to his dresser and opened the top drawer. He dug around underneath the socks until he felt the velvet box. Gripping it until he thought he might crush it, he walked to the bed and sat on the edge.

Slowly he lifted the lid. A diamond solitaire glinted under the overhead light. He wanted to look at it and remind himself how what seemed like love could go wrong. He'd planned to propose and give this diamond to Deanna when the stuff with Sydney shattered his life. He'd thought they were in love, but when Deanna believed the accusations against him, he'd realized that they hadn't truly known each other at all.

Now he thought Brittany could be the one, but what if he was wrong again? He didn't know how to deal with the situation. Not only did their relationship as employer and employee make things awkward, but, despite all the changes he'd made in his life in recent weeks, he still hadn't done the one thing he knew she needed him to do—forgive the people who had wronged him. That would stand in the way of giving Brittany the kind of love she deserved. He loved her, but that didn't seem like enough.

"Daddy?"

Parker looked up to find Rose standing in his bedroom doorway, Jasmine right behind her. He quickly snapped the case shut and got up. He walked over and laid it on the dresser.

"What are you girls doing down here? Didn't Brittany and I just put you to bed?" He ushered the girls into the rec room.

"Yes, but we've got something really important to ask you." Rose put a hand on one hip and gave him a matter-of-fact look.

"Why didn't you ask me when I put you to bed?"

"We couldn't because Brittany would hear."

"Why couldn't Brittany hear?"

"Cuz we want to know what we should get Brittany for her birthday." Jasmine tugged on one of his arms. "We want to get her something really good."

"How do you know about her birthday?"

"She got a birthday card, and she put it on her refrigerator."

"Do you know what day it is?"

"She said it's on Saturday. And she told us she's going to be twenty-six. That's old."

For a moment Parker pressed his lips together to keep from laughing. "Did you say that to her?"

Rose shook her head. "Delia told us it's not nice to tell people they're old."

"What did I tell you?" Carrying a basket full of towels, Delia came down the stairs.

"You said not to tell people they're old." Rose looked satisfied with herself.

"True, especially when you're talking about me." Laughing, Delia set the basket on the nearby couch and started folding the towels. "How did you get on this topic?"

"The girls were asking me what they can get Brittany for her birthday. They found out that it's this Saturday." Parker patted the girls on their heads.

"Guess that means I'm going to have to bake a birthday cake. Are we planning a party?"

Rose and Jasmine started jumping up and down. "Yeah. A party. A big party."

Parker looked at his overexcited daughters and held up one hand. "Wait a minute. She might have plans."

Rose turned to Jasmine. "We can ask her when we go to church tomorrow."

"Daddy, you can come with us." Jasmine stared up at him.

"I can't. I have a work deadline." Thankfully, he had that excuse. Now that they were attending church with Brittany, would they expect him to go? There was no way he could explain his aversion to church attendance—at least in Stockton.

"We can ask her about a party, can't we?" Jasmine tugged on his arm. "But what present can we get her?"

Delia put the last folded towel in the basket. "I have an idea."

Parker looked her way. "You do?"

"A dog. And I know where you can get one."

"Brittany loves dogs. She has them all over her house, but they're not real." Rose pulled on Parker's arm. "Can we get her a real dog, please?"

Parker knew the caution about getting people pets unless they wanted them. "She told me she wanted a dog when she was a kid, but that doesn't necessarily mean she wants one now."

"She already adores this dog," Delia said.

"How do you know?"

Delia looked at him as though she wasn't quite sure she should answer his question. "Last Sunday after church, we ate lunch over at the Prescotts' house."

"You never mentioned that." Parker certainly didn't want to discuss his problems with those folks in front of Rose and Jasmine. Larry Prescott had been one of Parker's best friends until the accusation against him. His former friend had turned his back like all the others.

"I didn't figure you wanted to hear about it. Anyway, while we were there, Brittany couldn't get enough of playing with their coonhound."

"If the dog belongs to the Prescotts, how does that help us get Brittany a dog?"

"That's just it. They have to get rid of the dog because their son, David, started having respiratory problems and sinus infections. They discovered that he's allergic to dogs, and they're looking for a good home for Bogey."

"Bogey?"

"Humphrey Bogart, to be exact." Delia laughed.

Parker smiled. "Bogey sounds like a good nickname."

"Daddy, you can get the dog, and Jas and I will plan the party." Rose grabbed Jasmine's hands and they jumped around in a circle.

"All right, let's calm down. No party planning tonight. You have to go to bed. Delia can help you make plans tomorrow." Parker motioned toward the stairway. "Now back to bed."

The girls scrambled up the stairs, chattering about Brittany's party. Parker drank in their excitement. He wanted to make Brittany happy, too, but he was afraid he would always fall short.

After Rose and Jasmine were safely tucked into their beds again, Parker moseyed into the kitchen and found Delia already planning the party menu. "Guess Rose and Jasmine aren't the only ones who are eager to have a party for Brittany."

"That girl deserves the best party we can give her. She's brought so much joy to your daughters." She gave him one of her famous no-nonsense stares. "And even to you."

"What's that supposed to mean?"

"I think you have an idea."

Parker decided to leave Delia's comment alone. He didn't want to discuss Brittany with Delia. The older woman knew him too well. "Well, since you seem to know what to do. Tell me how I'm supposed to get that dog from the Prescotts."

"Call them up."

"Sure. Just like that." Parker snapped his fingers. "They're going to let me have that dog. They'll probably think I'll abuse it."

Delia shook her head. "Most of the people in that church are sorry about what happened, especially Larry Prescott. They would welcome you with open arms, but you're the one who can't forget or forgive."

"Please don't lecture me."

"I'm not lecturing you—just giving you the facts." Delia stepped closer and poked an index finger at his chest. "If you love that girl, you'll do whatever it takes to get that dog."

"What makes you say I'm in love with her?"

"I see it every time you look at her."

Parker steeled himself against her words even though she was right. "You may be right, but there's not much I can do about it."

Delia waved a hand in the air. "What do you mean you can't do anything about it? Sure you can. You can give her the dog and tell her how you feel."

Hoping to avoid Delia's lecturing, Parker turned toward the window that looked out over the backyard where the moonlight illuminated the few patches of snow that remained. Spring was coming—a time of renewal, but Parker didn't feel anything except despair. "I can't ask her to love me."

"You don't have to ask her to love you. She already does."

Parker shook his head. "What makes you say that?"

Delia came around to face him. "The same way I can tell that you love her, I can see that she loves you. The two of you have been trying to deny what is so obvious to the rest of us."

Parker wanted to believe what Delia said, but he feared

the hurt if it wasn't true. Was he ready to take another chance on love? Minutes ago, he was looking at the ring and trying to convince himself that love wasn't for him. He knew Brittany cared about him and wanted him to get over the past. Did he love her enough to really try? Was the reward worth the risk? "I wish I could believe you."

"Believe me. I've kept quiet while you've hidden yourself away on this ranch, but I'm going to speak my piece now. I'm not going to let you throw away this chance at happiness because you're not willing to face your fears, to face the people who hurt you and forgive them. I love you as if you were my own son, and I hate what you've been doing to yourself. Bitterness eats away at you over time."

Parker stood there and blinked his eyes to make sure the woman standing before him was Delia. In all the years he'd known her, he'd never heard her speak so emphatically. She'd aimed her words at him and hit him right in the heart. He wasn't sure what to say. Maybe nothing.

She stared back at him. She walked over to the phone and picked up the receiver. "Call the Prescotts and ask about the dog."

"Are you sure they'll talk to me?"

Delia nodded as she held out the phone. "I don't see why not. You're the one who's built this barrier up in your mind over the years, not them."

Parker took the phone. A kick in the rear end was what he needed, and Delia had given it to him. "Do you have the number?"

"Right here." She pulled a piece of paper out of the desk drawer and slid it along the counter until it was right in front of him. Crossing her arms at her waist, she fixed her eyes on him. She was going to make sure he followed through.

He swallowed hard and stared at the paper. Would giving

Brittany a dog for her birthday help him win her love? Maybe, but even if Delia was right, he would have to come to grips with his past. He'd have to stop isolating himself on this ranch. If he wanted to share in her life, he was going to have to take that one big step that said *I'm ready to face the world again—face all those people who hurt me.*

Delia had just given him that opportunity. Could he do it? Did he have the courage to conquer his own fear? He picked up the phone. He would do this for Brittany.

His heart beat like a horse's hooves pounding across the ranch as he punched in the number. With each ring, his heart beat faster. When a male voice sounded on the other end, Parker's mouth was as dry as a Montana summer. He licked his lips. "Hello, this is Parker Watson. I'd like to speak to Larry Prescott."

For what seemed like a century, there was silence on the other end. Parker swallowed the lump in his throat that had reappeared. His palms grew sweaty. Maybe Delia had been wrong.

"Wow, Parker. You're the last person I expected to hear from today." Surprise, not animosity accented every syllable. "What can I do for you?"

"I understand that you're looking for a good home for a coonhound." Parker took a deep breath.

"We are. Are you interested?"

"Yeah, when can I come and see the dog?"

"Any evening. I get home from work about six."

"Tomorrow evening at six?" Parker knew he had to do it soon or he'd chicken out.

"Sure. I'll see you then."

Parker hung up the phone and turned to Delia. "I think you should pray for me."

Delia smiled. "I've been doing that for a long time. Seems like God is beginning to answer those prayers."

"I hope so because I'm going to need a lot of help." Hugging Delia, Parker couldn't believe he was asking someone to pray for him. All because of Brittany. She was changing his life.

Chapter Thirteen

Parker pulled into the driveway and shut off the engine as he stared at the cedar-sided ranch house where Larry Prescott lived. Parker had been in that house many times. He and Larry used to hunt and fish together. They had worked together, helping with the teen activities at church. But that had come to an end when the elders in the church decided they didn't want Parker around the youth group anymore.

Was Larry sorry about the way he'd treated Parker? Larry had never made an attempt to defend Parker. His former friend had remained silent while people destroyed Parker's reputation. He still remembered the angry, harsh words that he and Larry had exchanged. Could all of that be undone?

Parker got out of his vehicle and strode to the door before he changed his mind. First, making the trip to Stockton to get Valentine's gifts, then eating at the Steakhouse and now facing an estranged friend—all the things he'd done because he was falling in love with a cute little redhead. She was definitely making him a better man.

A boy of about twelve answered the door. Parker's pulse hammered in his head. Wow. Was this David? He hardly looked like the same kid who'd been about the same age as the girls were now the last time Parker had seen him.

A moment later Larry appeared in the doorway. "Come on in."

Parker stepped inside, unsure of what he should say. An awkward silence ensued until Larry's wife, Allison, walked into the room.

"Hi, Parker. Larry tells me you're interested in Bogey."

"Hello, Allison." Parker nodded. "I'd like to check him out."

Allison turned to David. "Go get Bogey."

After the boy sprinted out of the room, Larry finally spoke. "He loves that dog. And Allison and I have become pretty attached to Bogey, too. So it's kind of hard to give him up."

"I understand." Parker still wasn't sure how to react to meeting his former friends. They were talking to him as if nothing had ever happened—or even worse, as if they were strangers. No "I'm glad to see you again." No "I'm sorry about what happened."

Were they not going to acknowledge the fact that they hadn't seen each other in over six years? If that's the way they wanted it, he wasn't going to say anything. He'd take care of business and be on his way. Nothing had changed. These people still weren't ready to accept him. And he wasn't ready to forgive if they weren't going to offer so much as an apology.

When David returned, he commanded the dog to sit. Immediately, Bogey lowered his hindquarters to the floor. Parker hunkered down and held out his hand for the dog to sniff, then patted his head. The dog's tail thumped on the floor. At least he was friendly.

David told Bogey to stay, and he sat there like a statue. "He's really good with commands. I took him to obedience school."

"You've done a good job with him." Some of the tension

finally drained from Parker's body as he smiled at David. "Do you suppose he'll obey me if I give him a command?"

David nodded. "Go ahead."

"Bogey, lie down."

The dog lay down and stared up at Parker with sad eyes, almost as if he realized he was going to lose his young master.

"Let's see if he'll come to me." Parker walked to the other side of the room. "Come, Bogey."

Bogey could hardly wait to get to Parker's side. The dog's tail thumped on the floor again as he sat beside Parker. No wonder Brittany had taken to this dog. Parker could hardly wait until Saturday. He hoped she welcomed this surprise.

Parker glanced at Larry, who stood stoically beside Allison. "I'd like to take the dog. What do I owe you for him?"

"Nothing. He's yours."

"No. I'm prepared to pay you whatever he cost you." Parker pulled a checkbook out of a pocket in the inside of his jacket.

Larry stared at him for several seconds, then opened his mouth, but closed it again without saying anything.

"I can't take the dog without paying you for him."

Larry's shoulders slumped as he took a deep breath. "I want you to have the dog to make up for the terrible way I treated you. I'm sorry. You didn't deserve what happened to you."

The words Parker had wanted to hear from somebody, anybody in Stockton for six years, caused tightness in his chest. For a moment he couldn't speak as he swallowed the lump that had formed in his throat. "You're the first to say so. It's been hard to deal with people here. They never greet me or look me in the eye when we cross paths."

Larry nodded. "It's because they didn't know what to say to you. I know that's how I felt when you first walked into the house. How could I apologize? What could I possibly say to make up for my wrongheaded thinking?"

Parker shrugged, not sure how to respond himself. He'd carried around this bitterness for too many years to make everything right in a matter of minutes. The apology helped— but he wasn't ready to say all was forgiven. Not yet. "I still want to pay for the dog. I'm getting him as a birthday gift for a friend."

"Okay, how about if we compromise. You can pay me half of what he cost us. Two hundred and fifty dollars." Larry finally smiled.

Parker shook his head. "That's still too generous. I know how expensive a purebred hound can be. How about $350?"

"Three hundred." Larry gave him a pointed look that told Parker that he should take the offer.

"Deal." Parker held out his hand. "This is the first time I've ever negotiated to pay more for something."

Larry shook Parker's hand and didn't let go. "It's been too long. I should never have let this many years go by without trying to make amends. I hope someday you can forgive me."

Standing back, Parker gazed at Larry. That was the heart of the matter—finding a way to forgive. "I appreciate your apology, but I'm still working on the forgiveness. Today's a first step."

"I understand." Larry clapped Parker on the back. "There are a lot of people real sorry about the way we treated you. We sure would like to see you back in church again."

"I'll think about it." Some of the burden on his heart had lifted—one more good thing Brittany had brought to his life.

The phone jangled. Brittany picked up the receiver. "Hello."

"Happy birthday."

"Thanks, Dad. How are you?"

"Good."

A second later, Brittany's mom joined the conversation. They talked about her brothers, who were both in college, and the weather and the latest news from Pinecrest.

"Any big plans for the day?" her dad asked.

"Rose and Jasmine are having a party for me this afternoon. They can hardly contain their excitement. Those little girls are so full of life."

"Wish we could be there to celebrate with you, too." Her dad cleared his throat. "I've got some news about a job."

Brittany's stomach did a little flip-flop. "What?"

"I've been passing out your resume whenever I have a chance. The other day at lunch, I gave it to someone who read it and is very interested in having a phone interview with you. I told him I'd see when you were available."

Brittany didn't know what to say. When she'd first arrived on the ranch, she'd spent hours sending out her resume without any success. In the past couple of weeks, she hadn't even thought about looking for another job. She'd found contentment here, teaching two little girls. "What kind of a job?"

"In the accounting department of a finance company in Spokane. I thought it sounded perfect for you."

"You'll be closer to home. That would make me very happy." Her mother's voice resonated with eagerness.

Home. The word stood out in her mind. She hadn't thought of Pinecrest as home in weeks. She thought of the ranch as home. When had that happened? When Parker had unknowingly seized her heart? Silly question.

She knew the exact moment when she'd started falling in love with him. The scene came back to her in a flash— when he'd walked into that rental house carrying Rose and Jasmine like sacks of potatoes. Right then, he'd captured a little piece of her heart, and every day since then, he'd taken a little bit more until he had the whole thing. But did they have any chance of a future together? As much as she loved Parker, she knew he wouldn't be able to have a real relationship until he let go of the past.

She swallowed hard. "I don't know, Dad. Unless the man wants to call me on the weekends or in the evenings, I'm pretty tied up. Even when I'm not doing lessons, I'm still watching Rose and Jasmine. It would be kind of hard to talk with someone while they're around."

"Let me see what he says. He was very interested in talking to you. He was impressed with your resume."

Would it hurt to check it out? Just because she spoke with the man didn't mean he would offer her a job or that she would take it if he did. "Okay, Dad."

"Good. Have a great birthday. We love you."

"Love you, too. 'Bye."

Throughout the rest of the morning Brittany received calls from Heather, a couple of other friends from Billings and her brothers. Seconds after she finished talking with her younger brother, the phone rang again.

As soon as she picked up the receiver, giggles sounded on the other end. "Happy birthday."

"Thank you." The excited little voices touched her deep inside. How could she think of leaving these kids—or their father? She couldn't, but she'd told her dad she'd talk to the man. So she would. The whole thing could end there.

"Your phone kept being busy, and Daddy said we shouldn't bother you, but we called anyway."

"I was talking with my family and friends. They were wishing me a happy birthday."

"We're helping Delia make your cake."

"We made you cards."

"We know you're going to like your presents."

Brittany had no idea who was speaking as the girls talked

over each other. Then she heard a commotion in the background and some muffled words.

"Happy birthday."

Brittany's heart skipped a beat at the sound of Parker's voice. "Thanks. I hear I have a cake, cards and presents."

"You do, and I'm sorry about the girls disturbing you."

"They didn't disturb me. I like having people wish me happy birthday."

"We'll see you this afternoon for a lot more birthday wishes. Two o'clock."

"Okay. See you then." Brittany hung up the phone. This was going to be a much better birthday than last year—the one that Max had forgotten.

Rose and Jasmine nearly tackled Brittany when she walked through the front door of Parker's house. She hunkered down and hugged them back. They each took one of her hands and pulled her through the kitchen.

Rose looked up at her. "We're having the party downstairs."

"Follow us." Jasmine opened the door that led to the basement.

Rose and Jasmine clomped down the stairs. When they reached the bottom, Jasmine turned to Brittany. "Stop. You have to close your eyes. And no peeking."

"Okay." Smiling, Brittany closed her eyes and wondered what surprises the little girls had in store for her.

Rose and Jasmine led Brittany forward and stopped.

They let go of Brittany's hands. "You can open your eyes now."

As soon as she opened her eyes a loud chorus of happy birthdays rang through the air. She looked over the joyful group, and much to her surprise, had to blink back a few tears as her emotions overcame her. Finally, she noticed the huge banner plastered against one wall that read *Happy Birthday, Brittany.* A cake loaded with candles sat on a table in the corner. She had expected Parker, Delia and the girls to attend her party, but she hadn't expected everyone on the ranch.

Placing a hand over her heart, she couldn't stop grinning. "This is a surprise. Thanks, everyone."

From across the room, Parker smiled at her, and for an instant, despite the noisy greetings that swirled around them, Brittany felt as if they were the only two people in the room. Did he feel that connection, too? Or was it all in her imagination?

"You have to see your cards and presents." Rose's announcement pulled Brittany's attention away from Parker.

"Okay." As Brittany took her place of honor on the couch, she once again found Parker looking at her when she glanced in his direction. Her heart fluttered. He smiled almost as if he knew something she didn't.

Joyful comments and laughter filled the room as Brittany opened the cards and gifts one by one. Rose had made Brittany a potpourri ball to hang in her closet. Jasmine gave Brittany a paperweight she'd made. Delia had knit a scarf for her, and Derek and Christine presented her with a book. The cowhands had pitched in and gotten her a gift certificate from a women's shop in Stockton. And there were a few gag gifts thrown in for good measure.

Finally, Brittany opened Parker's gift, a collection of different kinds of hot chocolates and teas. He remembered that she didn't like coffee, and that made her smile.

"Open this one." Jasmine handed her the last remaining gift. "That's from Daddy, too."

Brittany opened the box and pulled the tissue-wrapped object out. When she removed the paper, she started laughing. She held up the mug that read, Crazy Dog Lady. She looked at Parker. "Am I supposed to drink out of this or add it to my dog collection?"

Grinning, Parker shrugged. "Whichever you'd like."

"This has been wonderful. Thank you so much."

"We have to have cake now." Rose pranced over to the table where the cake sat. "Daddy has to light the candles."

"Okay, birthday girl, can you blow out all the candles?" Parker waved her over as he finished lighting them.

As she made her way across the room, the group sang "Happy Birthday."

Brittany stared at the dancing flames and wondered whether she should make a wish. All her wishes lately revolved around Parker. She wished he'd find a way to get over his past hurts. She wished he'd come to church with the girls and her. She wished he could love her as she loved him. Too many wishes for one birthday cake. If she could only have one, she would wish that he would let God back into his life. She should stop wishing and start praying.

Finally, she took a big breath and blew. In a matter of seconds, not a flame was still burning. Applause and laughter sounded in her ears as Parker put an arm around her shoulders. With him standing so close, she almost forgot to breathe. She looked up at him. "I did it."

"You did." He grinned at her. "I hope you get your wish."

"Me, too." If only he knew what her wish had been.

Delia cut the cake, and Rose and Jasmine served. They played some silly games. A couple of the cowboys had to leave to check on the cows that were ready to give birth. A while later, after the games were over, the other guests had to leave, too. Everyone walked upstairs.

While they were getting on their coats, one of the cowboys who'd left earlier came rushing around the corner from the mudroom. "Hey, everyone, another gift for Brittany has arrived."

Knitting her eyebrows, she looked at Parker. He gave her this mischievous smile as Rose and Jasmine raced toward the mudroom.

Parker held up one hand. "Stay right here while I go check this out."

Brittany didn't miss the conspiratorial look that passed between Parker and the cowboy who'd announced the news. What was going on? She glanced around the group. From the looks on their faces, Brittany was pretty sure she was the only one who didn't know about this gift. Then she heard a dog bray. Her heart pounded, and she looked toward the door again.

Parker, Rose and Jasmine stood there holding the leash of a black-and-tan dog with a big hot-pink bow tied around his neck. "Happy birthday."

Brittany couldn't make her mouth form any words. She stood there looking at the threesome and the dog who sat so still, waiting for a command to move.

"Do you like him?" Rose ran over to Brittany.

"It's Bogey. Remember him?" Jasmine hurried over, leaving Parker with the dog that still hadn't moved one inch. "He's yours."

"Mine?" This time the tears of joy that had been all too close to the surface today came streaming down her cheeks. "My very own dog."

Parker unhooked the lead from the dog's collar. "Call him."

Brittany wiped her tears. "Come, Bogey."

The dog sprang forward and came to a stop in front of her. He wagged his tail so hard that it looked like the tail was wagging his body. Brittany laughed as she hunkered down and hugged the dog's neck. "Bogey, you are the perfect birthday present."

The dog barked, and everyone laughed. Standing, Brittany told Bogey to sit. The dog obeyed immediately. He sat there, his tail thumping the floor, as everyone said goodbye and wished Brittany well. After the last guest had left, Brittany turned to Parker. "How long have you had this dog?"

"Since Tuesday. The guys in the bunkhouse have been keeping him."

Brittany glanced at the girls, then looked back at Parker. "How did you ever keep Rose and Jasmine from spilling the secret?"

Rose scrunched up her face. "We're good at keeping secrets."

"We didn't tell anyone." Jasmine shook her head.

Brittany leaned over and hugged Rose and Jasmine. "Thank you."

"Hug Daddy, too." Rose pointed at Parker. "He's the one who got Bogey for you."

Her heart beating in rhythm with the dog's tail, Brittany met Parker's gaze. Winking, he gave her a lopsided grin. He knew what the girls were up to as well as she did, but Brittany didn't mind at all.

As she hugged Parker, Brittany knew she could get used to being in his arms. She wondered how long she could keep her own secret that she loved him.

When she stepped out of his embrace, he winked again. "I'll have to give you a dog every day."

In a flash Brittany thought about this morning's conversation with her dad. The job prospect. Now that Bogey was hers could she even consider leaving? She didn't want another job, but maybe Parker would never love her the way she loved him. She pushed the conflicting thoughts out of her mind. Chances were that nothing would come of the phone interview anyway. She didn't want to dissect her relationship with Parker now. She just wanted to enjoy her birthday.

"Girls, we have to clean up." Delia reached into the pantry and pulled out a big trash bag.

Rose and Jasmine scrambled after Delia as she led the way across the kitchen to the stairway. The girls went by her when she stopped and looked at Brittany. "You're staying for supper. I'm fixing one of your favorites—pot roast with mashed potatoes and gravy."

"Oh, that sounds good. Thank you." Brittany took a step toward them. "I can help straighten up."

"No, this is your birthday." Delia waved her away. "You go relax. Get to know your dog."

Parker strode over to Delia. "I'll take the trash bag and supervise the cleanup. That way you'll have a chance to relax with Brittany before you have to start supper."

"I'll take you up on that. Thanks." Smiling, Delia handed the trash bag to Parker, then looked at Brittany. "Come into the den, and I'll show you the throw I'm knitting."

Bogey followed them and lay on the floor beside Brittany's feet. She reached down and took the bow off the dog's collar. Delia put on her glasses and picked up the throw from her knitting basket. She held it up for Brittany to see.

"That's beautiful."

"Thanks." Delia looked over her glasses at the dog. "I think Bogey's already taken to his new owner."

Brittany put one hand over her heart and patted Bogey's head with the other. "He's a terrific dog. I knew it the first time we went to the Prescotts. I can't believe he's mine. Do you know how this happened?"

Delia told Brittany the whole story. After she finished, she looked Brittany in the eye. "I hope you realize what it took for Parker to get that dog for you."

Brittany nodded, a myriad of emotions welling up inside her. She lowered her gaze and stroked Bogey's head as she tried to regain her composure. She finally looked up. "Thanks for sharing that. I'm beginning to understand what he's been through."

Delia touched Brittany's arm. "He cares about you. Please give him time to find the strength to forgive all those people."

"I wish I could make it happen now."

Delia nodded. "Me, too. I'm praying every day."

Before Brittany could respond, Rose and Jasmine charged into the room. Rose plopped onto the couch beside Brittany. "We're done cleaning."

"We brought up the leftover cake." Jasmine joined them on the couch.

A second later Parker appeared in the doorway and looked at Brittany. "Would you like to take Bogey for a walk?"

"Yeah." Both girls jumped up.

While they walked, the girls skipped ahead, their pigtails bouncing around their shoulders. Parker reached over and took her hand, and he smiled down at her. She felt the warmth of his hand even through the gloves they wore. Contentment settled around her heart. Was Parker finding the peace he needed? She hoped so.

When they returned from the walk, the girls and Parker set the table. Soon they were seated, and Jasmine gave thanks for the food. After they ate and cleaned up the kitchen, the evening fell into a familiar routine—games, a story, then bedtime for the girls. During the whole evening Bogey was never far from Brittany's side.

As they left Rose and Jasmine's room, Parker gazed down at her. "Looks like you have a constant shadow. I can't believe how quickly that dog adopted you."

Brittany gave him an impish grin. "It's my lovable nature. He recognized it the moment we met."

"Smart dog." Parker put his arm around her shoulders. "I ordered a chick flick just for your birthday. I hope you're planning to stay and watch it."

Brittany laughed. "You'd suffer through a chick flick for me?"

He nodded slowly. "Today's your day."

Was today a new beginning for him? She wanted to believe it was. As they watched the movie, Brittany wondered whether she was putting too much stock in Parker's actions.

After the movie was over, Parker loaded all of Bogey's food and supplies in his SUV, then drove Brittany and her new dog home. When Parker opened the back door, Bogey bounded out of the backseat and sniffed his way to the front door, then followed Brittany as she and Parker unloaded the dog supplies.

When they were finished, Brittany stood on the front porch with Parker and Bogey. "Thanks for everything. I'll always remember this birthday."

Parker stood there without speaking, his eyes focused on her as he leaned closer. When Brittany recognized the look, her heart bumped up its rhythm. He was going to kiss her.

"I hope you'll always remember this." Parker pulled her into his arms and kissed her.

As his lips met hers, Brittany was sure the little patch of snow beside the house must be melting. She savored his kiss—a kiss that she didn't want to end. She knew this was going to change everything between them.

Bogey whined, and Parker released her. "Hey, Bogey, you're not jealous, are you? You gotta learn to share."

Brittany laughed, and Parker pulled her close again and held her. "You're the best thing that's happened to me in a long time. I love you. You make me want to be a better person, but I'm not there yet. Will you be patient with me?"

She nodded. He loved her. That should make her happy, but she still feared that love wasn't enough to resolve the issues that stood between them. She loved the Lord, but

Parker held Him at arm's length. "I love you, too. I care about you."

If he wanted to be a better person, did she dare push? She remembered how angry he'd gotten when she'd asked him to let Rose and Jasmine go to Stockton with her. But then he'd changed his mind and said they could go. Maybe all he needed was a little nudge to make him join the girls and her at church.

"Parker?"

He stepped away and looked at her. "I know that look. Don't ask me because I don't want to have to turn you down on your birthday."

When she opened her mouth, he gently put his index finger across her lips. She closed her eyes, her heart sinking. Was she too impatient? "Okay, I won't ask tonight, but someday I will. I hope you can say yes."

He didn't say anything else, just gave her a peck on the cheek and sprinted to his vehicle. She patted Bogey's head as she watched Parker drive away, taking her heart with him.

Chapter Fourteen

What did she do now? With a heavy sigh, Brittany hung up the phone. The manager at the finance company, Mr. Hughes, had called to let her know they wanted to do an in-person interview with her. Last week's phone interview had put her in the running for the position, along with two other candidates. She should be thrilled.

Despite her love for Parker and his little girls, Brittany was torn. She wanted to please her dad, too. After all, he'd gone to a lot of trouble to get these people to look at her resume. What if they offered her the job? Could she turn it down? How could she explain that decision to her parents? *Oh, I don't want the job because I'm hoping the man I work for now will find a way to get over his bitterness and ask me to marry him.* If she told them that, they would think she'd lost her mind. Maybe she had. She'd definitely lost her heart.

She glanced down at Bogey. He looked up at her as if he understood her dilemma. She didn't want to leave Parker or Rose and Jasmine. The decision should be easy. So why wasn't it?

She'd told Mr. Hughes that she would have to make arrangements to get off work and that she would call back on Monday evening to let him know when she could come for the interview. She had the whole weekend to think things over. That bought her some time—time to figure out what she was going to say to Parker. From the very beginning she'd let him know she would be looking for a job in the field of finance. Would her decision surprise him? Would it cause him to rethink his position on renewing his faith and attending church?

She was falling in love with Parker more every day, but he still had a past that haunted him—kept him from being the man he should be. She thought when he'd gotten the dog for her that maybe he'd realize that the people at church wanted forgiveness for the way they'd treated him, but he refused to see it.

He hung onto the bitterness like a life raft in the sea of his own disappointments. He said he loved her, but not enough to make that change in his life. Shades of Max. Max had said he loved her, but he couldn't change, either. He always put her second to his studies and work.

She would have to tell Parker about the job interview. What would he say? She hated to leave, but maybe it was for the best. But telling Parker was the easy part. He was an adult, and he'd understand why she was doing this. But Rose and Jasmine. The thought of trying to explain this to them made her feel as though a crushing stone sat on her chest. Her stomach soured. Misery stared her in the face.

Brittany bowed her head, but she didn't know what to pray. Her thoughts swam around in her head like objects being sucked down a giant hole. She couldn't grasp one and hang onto it. *Lord, I don't know what to pray for. Please help me.*

While she sat there, Bogey at her feet, a tiny knock sounded on the door. Bogey barked. Giggles came from outside. Brittany would know those giggles anywhere. Had God sent her an answer already? No matter what their father did or didn't do, how could she consider leaving Rose and Jasmine?

Telling Bogey to stay, Brittany hurried to answer the door. Grinning, the two girls stood on the porch. They each held a blue plastic container. "Who's out here giggling on my porch?"

Rose giggled some more and held up her container. "We are. We brought you chocolate-chip cookies."

"Delia helped us make them." Jasmine handed her container to Brittany. "And we have treats for Bogey, too."

Brittany took the containers. "I can hardly wait to try them."

Bogey's tail thumped on the floor as the girls scrambled into the house.

"Bogey wants his, too." Jasmine patted the dog's head.

"Let's have a party." Rose danced around the room.

Jasmine shook her head. "Rose, Daddy told us we couldn't stay. We could only bring Brittany and Bogey the treats."

Brittany frowned. "Why did he say you couldn't stay?"

"He said today is your day off and we shouldn't bother you." Rose pressed her lips together as she looked up at Brittany.

Brittany wanted to say that was silly, but she didn't want to say anything bad about Parker to his girls. She would have to say it directly to him. "Well, I'm going to invite you to stay for cookies and milk. Then we'll take Bogey for a walk. We might even go over and say hi to your dad. What do you think?"

"Yay!" Rose and Jasmine clapped.

Bogey barked and wagged his tail.

"Bogey likes that idea, too." Rose giggled, then covered her mouth.

Brittany walked over to the phone. "I'll call Delia and let her know what we're doing."

After Brittany spoke to Delia, Rose and Jasmine helped set the small table in the schoolroom with plates and glasses. They even set a place for Bogey. Soon they were sharing cookies, milk and laughter. They finished their treats, then Brittany read them another chapter in the book she'd started. Bogey listened, too. Contentment wrapped around Brittany's heart.

Brittany closed the book. "Let's take Bogey for his walk."

Rose jumped up. "I get to hold his leash."

"I want to hold it." Jasmine pouted.

Brittany looked back and forth between the two girls. "Whose turn to go first?"

"Mine." Rose raised her hand.

Jasmine shook her head. "It's my turn."

Brittany tried to remain stern, but she almost laughed. A first. They'd forgotten who was supposed to go first, and Parker wasn't here to see it. "How are we going to decide this if you can't remember?"

Jasmine pointed to Brittany. "You pick."

Brittany wanted to avoid that scenario at all costs. "I'll do it this way. I'll write a number between one and ten on this piece of paper. You each write down a number, and whoever is closest will get to hold the leash first."

While Brittany and her charges wrote down their numbers, Bogey looked on with interest, his tail wagging. When everyone revealed their numbers, Jasmine had picked the number closest to Brittany's. They put on their coats, gloves and hats and were soon on their way down the lane toward the big house.

By the time they'd finished walking Bogey, each girl had taken a turn holding the leash. They'd forgotten about their disagreement by the time they reached home.

Rose picked up a stick lying in the yard. "Let's play fetch with Bogey."

Brittany nodded. "I think he'll like that."

Jasmine gave the dog a hug, then looked over at Rose. "You get to go first."

Brittany stood next to the garage and watched the kids and Bogey play. While she stood there, Parker came out the front door and walked over to her.

"Delia told me that you called and said the girls were staying with you for a while." He smiled, but raised his eyebrows. "You know today is your day off."

"I know, but I don't have anything else to do. Don't ruin my entertainment."

"You mean our regular Saturday night movie isn't enough entertainment for you?"

She gazed up at him. "You know I love watching movies with you, but I also like having cookies and milk with Rose and Jasmine. And Bogey enjoys their company, too. Rose and Jasmine sure love him." Brittany hunched her shoulders. "I have to tell you. They had their first disagreement about whose turn it was."

Parker chuckled, and Brittany proceeded to tell him how they resolved it.

"Good thinking." He gave her shoulders a little squeeze. "Gotta get back to work. Don't let those girls monopolize your time."

After Parker left, Rose and Jasmine played with Bogey until Delia called them in. Brittany looked at the girls as they hugged Bogey goodbye. Without saying a word, two little girls and a dog begged her to stay. How could she think of leaving even if Parker didn't make the changes she hoped for? She made her decision. She'd have to tell Mr. Hughes that she wouldn't be coming for the interview. And somehow she would have to make her parents understand.

* * *

"Parker, please come over."

Parker heard the tears in Brittany's voice. "Brittany, what's wrong?"

"It's my dad. He's had a heart attack. Please come now."

"I'll be right over."

After explaining the situation to Delia, Parker sprinted to Brittany's place. He didn't bother to knock, but went right in. "Brittany, I'm here."

She came out of the bedroom, and he immediately gathered her in his arms. "Is your dad going to be okay?"

She nodded. "He's stable for now, but I need to go home."

"Absolutely." Parker held her at arm's length as he gazed at her. "When did you find this out?"

Tears sprang to her eyes. "Just a few minutes ago. I got a call from my mom as I was finishing breakfast."

"Don't worry about anything here. Delia and I can cover the girls' lessons until you get back."

Brittany took a shaky breath, and her brow furrowed. "That's just it. I might not be coming back."

Parker couldn't believe what he was hearing. Fear gripped his mind. "If your dad gets better, why won't you be coming back?"

Brittany lowered her eyes. "My dad helped me get this interview with a company in Spokane. I'd decided not to go through with it, but now I'm reconsidering."

"Reconsidering?"

"Yes. I've been praying about it." Brittany sighed. "I thought God was telling me to stay here, but now I'm not so sure. Maybe the reason I got the interview was so I'd be able to move back to Spokane and help take care of my dad."

"I think you're confused."

"I don't know. Even if I do the interview, I may not get the job, but I have to do this for my dad."

"What about us? Rose, Jasmine and me?"

"I don't know that, either. I'd tell you to pray about it, but you don't pray."

Parker took a calming breath. He hadn't been a praying man in a long time, though he was working on it. But he didn't want to argue with her. He loved her, and he was afraid he was going to lose her. She was upset right now, so there was no sense in trying to reason with her. He had to let her go.

Parker gently gripped her arms. "Don't make any decisions while you're upset."

"Please don't tell me what to do. I just want to get on the road."

"You're driving?"

"The airfares are out of sight, and the connections are terrible. If I drive I can leave today. If I fly, I can't leave until tomorrow."

Fear twisted his gut. She didn't want him giving her advice, but he hated thinking of her making the over five-hundred-mile trip alone in her old car. "I'm not trying to tell you what to do, but if you're going to drive, please use one of my vehicles."

"Is that how you intend to get me back here?" She inhaled a shaky breath.

Parker shook his head. "I want you to be safe, and your old car is hardly in shape for a long trip."

She nodded. "You're right. Thanks for the offer."

"I love you, and I want you to come back." He wanted so badly to hold her in his arms.

She blinked, and a tear rolled down her cheek. She wiped it away as she shook her head. "I don't know. I want to come back, but maybe our relationship isn't meant to be. I don't see how we can move forward unless you somehow resolve your bitterness."

"I'm working on it." He wanted to defend himself more strongly, but he hadn't taken that last step—the one that meant letting God back into his life completely. He hadn't even talked to Larry Prescott since the day he'd bought Bogey. "I thought you loved me and were willing to give me time to work through this."

"I do, but I can't think about it right now."

Parker knew this discussion would have to wait. He reached over and tilted her chin up with his index finger until she was looking right at him. "Just remember I love you. And remember this."

He took her in his arms and gently kissed her. When she didn't pull away, he pulled her closer. He wanted to hold her forever, but he knew he had to let her go—let her go to Spokane, knowing she might not return.

Parker went to get Rose and Jasmine, who'd been watching a movie when he'd left. Brittany would be here in a few minutes to drop off Bogey and say goodbye to them, and he wanted to prepare them for Brittany's sad news. He called the girls' names as he descended the stairs. They didn't respond.

When he entered the rec room, he heard little excited voices coming from his bedroom. They weren't allowed in there unless they asked permission. What had prompted them to go into his room?

Frowning, he tiptoed to the doorway. Rose and Jasmine had their heads together as they looked at something he couldn't see.

"What are you girls doing in here?"

The twosome jumped apart, and Jasmine put her hands behind her back. They hunched their shoulders as they looked everywhere around the room except at him.

"Nothing," Rose said, while Jasmine remained silent.

"Jas, what do you have behind your back?"

The little girl bit her lower lip and shook her head, then looked at her sister for help.

"Jas, please tell me what you and Rose are up to."

Jasmine wouldn't meet his gaze. "Rose said we should look at it."

"What are you looking at?"

Jasmine's lower lip began to tremble, and she burst into tears as she shoved the black velvet box at him.

Parker took it. The engagement ring. Why on earth did they have this? He looked from one child to the other. "You know you're not supposed to touch my things without permission."

They both nodded, still refusing to look him in the eye.

"I'm waiting for your explanation."

Finally, Jasmine looked up, tears welling in her big brown eyes. "We wanted to see it."

"And how did you know it was here?"

"We saw you looking at it."

Parker knit his eyebrows as he tried to think about when they would've seen it. Then he remembered the day he'd had it out to remind himself of Deanna's rejection. "Just because you saw me with it doesn't give you permission to look at it."

Jasmine pointed at Rose. "Rose said you were going to give it to Brittany when you asked her to marry you."

Stunned, Parker shook his head, not believing what Jasmine had said. Was his interest in Brittany that apparent to them, or was this wishful thinking on their part?

True, he loved Brittany and wanted to marry her, but he knew that wasn't going to happen yet. Maybe it never would. Two big problems kept them apart. How was he going to explain the whole mess to his little girls? Their sense of disappointment would be double.

"Girls, I want you to go sit on the couch in the rec room. We're going to have a talk."

"Okay." Rose and Jasmine left the room, dragging their feet.

Parker opened the case and looked at the ring. He wouldn't be giving this to anyone. If he ever asked Brittany to marry him, he would definitely get a new one for her. He tossed the case back in his sock drawer. Leaving it on the dresser had been a big mistake. If he'd put it away, Rose and Jasmine wouldn't have found it, and he wouldn't be facing two explanations.

Not looking forward to the upcoming conversation, he plodded into the rec room. Rose and Jasmine sat quietly on the couch, their little legs sticking straight out as they had their backs pressed to the cushions behind them. He loved his children so much that sometimes it hurt. It hurt to give them bad news. He wanted to make everything smooth for them, but life didn't work that way.

He sat down on the oak coffee table in front of the couch and looked at their expectant faces. Where did he start? Probably with the ring. "Girls, that ring is for no one."

Rose scooted forward. "Then why do you have it?"

"I bought it for someone a long time ago...before you were born."

"How come that person doesn't have it?" Jasmine knit her little eyebrows.

"I was dating a lady, and I wanted to marry her, but she didn't want to marry me."

"Brittany will marry you, and you can give her the ring." Rose bobbed her head.

"No, Rose, I'm not going to ask Brittany to marry me."

"But you love her."

"She's our friend, and we love our friends." Parker took a deep breath. He hoped they would understand. "I've got some bad news about Brittany."

"Is she sick?" Concern painted Jasmine's face.

"No, but her dad is. He's in the hospital, and Brittany has to go to see him today. She's coming in a few minutes to say goodbye and leave Bogey with us." Parker paused. He didn't want to say the next part, but it had to be said. "And she might not come back."

"I'll pray so her dad will get better. Then she can come back." Rose clasped her hands as if she was going to start praying right that minute.

"That's a good idea." Prayer was a good thing, but something he found hard to do. Maybe his girls could do it for him. But even if their prayers were answered and Brittany's dad got better, she might not come back because of that job prospect and because she was afraid he would never get over the past. He wasn't going to tell the girls that part.

Jasmine tapped him on the arm. "If Brittany's gone, who's going to take us to church and the Easter-egg hunt tomorrow?"

"I don't know. We'll get someone to do it." He wished Delia were able to drive, but the pain medication she took for her back meant she couldn't operate a car. Derek and Christine were going into Billings to see her parents for Easter, and the cowhands were busy watching the cows that were ready to give birth.

"You could take us."

"We'll see." Parker patted Jasmine on the head.

"You should go to church because it's Easter. That's the day Jesus came back to life so he could take away our sins."

Swallowing a lump in his throat, Parker nodded. His little girl was giving him a sermon in a nutshell. Could God take away his sin—the bitterness, the malevolent feelings he'd had for the people he used to worship with? At one time he thought so. Now he wasn't sure. He'd spent too many years despising those people.

He'd managed to get beyond some of it when he'd gone

to get Bogey. But he'd only had to talk to Larry Prescott and his family, not a whole congregation. Parker feared that he couldn't put his acrimony aside if he had to sit in church with the people who had condemned him. Could he ask God to help him overcome the animosity?

That night, as Parker stood in the doorway to his daughters' room with Bogey sitting at his side, he listened to their prayers. How many nights had Brittany been standing here with him? His mind replayed her sad goodbye this afternoon. He forced himself not to dwell on that now. He couldn't undo the past—none of it.

Rose's high-pitched little voice rang out. "Dear God, please help Brittany's dad get better so she can come back and be with us."

Seconds later, Jasmine's softer voice floated to him. "Dear God, thank You for our daddy and please let him marry Brittany. Then we can all be together."

His heart twisting, he avoided eye contact with Delia who'd laid out their clothes. He gave Rose and Jasmine a kiss and a hug, then escaped to the den where he had to play Easter bunny. He hoped Delia wouldn't mention his daughters' requests, but he was sure he would hear from her.

The girls had put their Easter baskets on the table in the den. While he was filling the baskets with chocolate bunnies and colorful eggs filled with goodies, he remembered Rose and Jasmine's prayers. Ever since Brittany had come into his life, he'd felt God's pull. Had God sent her to help him turn his life around? Had God made sure he'd heard his girls' prayers? Parker wanted to make Rose and Jasmine's wishes come true, but he wasn't sure he could.

Delia walked into the room and interrupted his thoughts. She set a bag on the table and eyed him. "Here are some things that Brittany left for you to put in the girls' baskets." Delia pointed a finger at him. "And what are you going to do about the thing those little girls want more than anything else?"

"What can I do?"

"I think you know." She nodded her head at him, then left him standing there with his guilt.

Before he went to bed, he slipped down the hallway and looked into the girls' room. Their night-light illuminated the room just enough so he could see their peaceful little faces. Then he caught a glimpse of the Easter dresses, the ones Brittany had made for them.

How could he disappoint his daughters? But how could he walk into that church and not feel animosity toward the people in the pews? Nothing was fair about two rotten choices.

Parker went to bed, but he couldn't sleep. So he went into the rec room and turned on the TV, not caring what was on. He wanted some noise—noise that might keep him from thinking about Brittany too much.

Bogey meandered over to the couch, laid his head on Parker's leg and looked up at him with those sad, soulful eyes. The dog had sat guard next to the mudroom door for most of the day, waiting for Brittany to return.

"I know what you mean, buddy. I miss her, too." Parker stroked Bogey's head. The dog whimpered. Parker could relate.

He'd spent countless hours on this ranch with only the girls and Delia for company. Now Brittany's absence would make the ranch a very lonely place. He already missed her smile, her laughter and the joy she'd brought into his life.

What was he going to do about it?

While he sat there feeling sorry for himself, the lyrics of a song playing on the TV caught his attention. "Forgiveness," the musician crooned. His heart hammering, he let the words of the song sink into his brain. The line about anger eating him up inside punched him in the gut.

His bitterness toward the people in Stockton had made his life miserable for six years. Isn't that what Brittany, and lately Delia, had been trying to tell him? Now a pop vocal group's song made him see the truth. Tomorrow morning he had to take the girls to church and rid himself of this anger. He bowed his head and prayed for forgiveness and that he would have the courage to forgive.

Chapter Fifteen

Muted conversation mingled with the sound of organ music as Parker stood at the back of the sanctuary. A man Parker didn't know greeted him with a smile, then gave him a bulletin. Fingering the paper, Parker swallowed hard and searched the crowd for Delia's distinctive Easter bonnet—a yellow, wide-brimmed affair with a big floppy flower on the front and a couple of feathers that poked off to the side. He'd kidded her about those feathers on the drive into Stockton in an attempt to calm his nerves.

Parker spotted the feathers waving in the air near the front. When he'd dropped Delia and the girls at the front door before parking, he should've known she would sit near the front. No way was he going to walk by all these people. He decided to sit on one of the chairs along the back wall.

Before he reached a chair, Larry Prescott approached, a grin on his face. He extended his hand. "Parker, you don't know how glad I am to see you."

His pulse pounding in his head, Parker shook Larry's hand. "Thanks."

"You by yourself?"

"Delia is up front, and Rose and Jasmine are in children's

church." Parker motioned toward the nearby chair. "But I'm going to sit here."

"Okay." Larry clapped Parker on the back. "See you after the service."

Parker nodded, and Larry joined his wife sitting in a pew halfway up the aisle. Parker expelled a harsh breath as he sat down. At least there was one friendly person in the crowd. Sitting in the back had its advantages. No one would be staring at him. The service started, and people stood to sing. The words to a familiar song flashed up on a big screen at the front. Parker joined the singing even though he hadn't sung a hymn in a long time. He was surprised at how good it felt.

The rest of the service, including the sermon, was a fog in Parker's mind because he spent most of the time praying. As he had the night before, he prayed that God would give him the courage to forgive and be forgiven. He prayed for Brittany's dad. He prayed that she would let him be part of her life—that she would come back to the ranch. Parker didn't know whether God would answer these prayers with the outcome that Parker wanted, but he knew God would answer them. A peace he hadn't felt in a long time surrounded his heart.

The pastor, new to the congregation since Parker had quit attending, ended his sermon with an invitation for anyone who wanted to turn his life over to God. Parker knew that meant him, but he couldn't make his feet move.

While he stood there wavering, Larry suddenly appeared and looked Parker right in the eyes. "I'm going up to ask for forgiveness for the way I treated you. Do you want to join me?"

Parker nodded and strode up the aisle alongside his friend. His friend. Yeah. He wanted to renew that friendship. When they reached the front, the minister spoke to them quietly about why they had come. Others came, as well. Some came for special prayers and others to rededicate their lives to God.

When the pastor came to Larry, he motioned for Parker to join him. With his head lowered, Parker stood beside Larry. He couldn't look out at the pews. He was afraid of what he might see.

Placing a hand on Parker's shoulder, Larry took the microphone. "Many of you know Parker Watson. He's a good man, and I'm here today to ask his forgiveness for the way I treated him. I hope you'll join me."

When Parker looked up, he saw a lot of surprised faces, but he saw a lot of smiles, too.

With God's help he would do this. He gathered his courage and reached for the microphone, his hand trembling. "I want to thank Larry for asking me to find my way back here. In recent days I've asked God to forgive me for the bitterness and anger I've carried around for the past six years. But God couldn't forgive me until I forgave the people who hurt me." Parker took a deep breath. "So I'm here today to say I'm going to put the past behind me, and I pray that you can do the same."

As Parker handed the microphone back to the minister, Delia's face beamed, and she wiped tears from her eyes. He smiled back at her. Making peace with God and the people around him made him feel good. He wished Brittany were also here to share in his redemption.

Parker stood at the front of the sanctuary while the minister closed the service with a prayer. When the prayer was over, Larry reached over and embraced Parker. "It's good to have you back, friend."

Parker nodded, not knowing whether he could speak. Soon he was surrounded by many in the congregation who expressed their thanks that he'd forgiven them for their wrongheadedness. While he stood there trying to take it all in, Delia pushed her way through the crowd and gave him a big hug, her feathers tickling his nose.

A few seconds later, Rose and Jasmine scooted through the crush. He hunkered down and hugged them. They didn't have any idea what had transpired, but they were going to be beneficiaries of the change in his attitude.

"Daddy, are you going to watch us in the Easter-egg hunt?" Rose pointed down the aisle. "It's going to be out there in a few minutes."

"Hurry. We don't want to miss the beginning." Jasmine took his hand.

Smiling, Parker looked over the folks surrounding him. "Thanks. I appreciate your acceptance and welcome." He glanced down at his girls, then back at the crowd. "Duty calls."

Goodhearted laughter followed him as Rose and Jasmine escorted him down the aisle. He shook hands with more well-wishers when he joined the parents who were assembled to watch the Easter-egg hunt on the church lawn on an unusually warm spring day. God had sent sunshine, as well as forgiveness to warm Parker's heart. As the children gathered with their baskets in hand, Delia, Larry and Allison joined Parker.

Again Larry shook Parker's hand. "You've done a world of good for this congregation."

Parker shrugged. "Don't give me any credit. If you hadn't come back and talked to me, I might not have walked down that aisle. Thanks."

Before Larry could respond, a whistle blew. The hunt had begun. Parents laughed and cheered while children dressed in their Easter finery roamed the church grounds looking for colorful plastic eggs filled with goodies. Parker smiled as he watched Rose and Jasmine scamper here and there, picking up eggs.

A cry split the air when a little girl fell and spilled the contents of her basket. Rose and Jasmine were there in a second and began helping the other child pick up the dropped eggs. Then they helped her find more. Warmth filled his chest as he took in their kindness. That was something Brittany had probably taught them.

Everything today seemed to bring Brittany to mind. The thought of her never coming back took away all the good feelings that the day had produced. He didn't want to live without her.

Now that he'd let God fill his heart with forgiveness, Parker knew he had one thing to do. Rose, Jasmine and he needed Brittany more than some finance company did. He had to see her and show her that he'd actually changed. He was determined to convince her to come back to the ranch and marry him.

Gripping Rose and Jasmine's hands, Parker stopped at the nurses' station to get directions to Dave Gorman's room.

Rose tugged on his hand. "Daddy, is that where Brittany is?"

Parker nodded. Their shoes clicked on the tile floor as they walked down the corridor in the direction the nurse had indicated.

"Will she get to go home with us?" Jasmine looked up at him.

"We'll have to see." Parker sighed. He didn't want to answer any more questions or make any promises about Brittany. He didn't know what to expect from her. He'd fielded his daughters' questions on the entire drive from the ranch to Spokane. In a few minutes he expected to get some answers.

Parker stopped in the hallway outside the door that stood ajar. Should he knock? Should he go in? Should he poke his head around the door? He didn't think he'd be this nervous or indecisive.

"May I help you?"

Parker turned to see a nurse coming out of the room across the hall. "Is it okay to go in?"

"I'll check for you." The nurse disappeared around the door.

As they waited, Parker was sure the sound of his heartbeat was echoing up and down the hall. His mouth felt like it was full of some of the gauze on the nearby cart.

The nurse returned. "You may go in. I told Mr. Gorman he has company."

Parker released a harsh breath, then strode through the doorway with Rose and Jasmine clinging to him.

Brittany stood by her father's bed. She turned, and the color drained from her face. "Parker, what—"

"Brittany." Rose and Jasmine dropped Parker's hands and charged toward Brittany. They enveloped her in a hug. "We missed you."

Parker's stomach churned as he looked at Brittany, then at her parents. "I'm sorry…"

"That's okay. Children can get excited." Brittany's mother, a petite dark haired woman, immediately walked over to him and extended her hand. "I'm Lori Gorman." She motioned toward the bed. "And this is my husband, Dave. And you must be Brittany's boss all the way from Montana. This *is* a surprise."

"I am." *Brittany's boss.* Had he made a mistake in coming here to propose? He wanted her to be a whole lot more than his employee. Parker turned to Brittany's dad. "I'm glad to meet you. How are you doing?"

Dave smoothed back a patch of thinning red hair. "Better. Thanks to a lot of prayer and some good docs. They tell me I'm going to be fine. Just have to take it easy for a while."

"That's good to hear." Parker's heart hammered as he turned to look at Brittany. She wasn't paying any attention to him. She was listening intently as Rose and Jasmine tried to talk over each other.

"Rose. Jasmine. Give Brittany a break." When the trio jerked their heads in his direction, he realized how harsh his words sounded.

Brittany hugged the girls to her. "That's okay. They were telling me how well they've been taking care of Bogey."

"They've done a good job." Now what did he say? He wanted to talk to Brittany alone. How was he going to accomplish that?

Rose skipped over to the bed and peered at Dave. "I'm Rose. Are you Brittany's daddy?"

"And I'm Jasmine." Jasmine shuffled up next to Rose.

Dave smiled. "Yes, I'm Brittany's daddy, and I'm glad to meet you. Brittany has told us a lot about you."

Rose moved closer to the bed. "I prayed lots for you."

"Me, too."

"Thank you."

Rose got a very serious expression on her face. "You know what?"

"What?" Dave continued to smile as he looked at Rose.

"We drove all the way here, so my daddy could ask Brittany to marry him. Then she can come back to the ranch and be our mommy."

The beeping of the heart monitor sounded loud in the otherwise silent room. Brittany stared at Parker in disbelief. Her parents looked at him with their mouths open, then immediately clamped them shut.

"Isn't that good news?" Jasmine's cheery little voice broke the stunned silence.

Rose tapped Lori on the arm. "That will make you my grandma."

Lori's eyes twinkled. "Well, I think you're right."

Parker couldn't move. His shoes might as well have been glued to the floor. How was he going to undo the mess his kids had made? They'd embarrassed Brittany, her parents and him.

Finally, he got up enough courage to look at Brittany. "Can we talk?"

"Go. I'll watch these precious little girls." Lori waved Brittany toward the door.

What must Brittany think? Trying to recall even one sentence of the speech he'd practiced, Parker went into the hallway. Nothing was coming back to him.

When he looked up, Brittany stood there smiling. She closed the gap between them, put her arms around his neck and kissed him.

Parker stepped back. "Why...? How...?"

Her eyes shimmering with tears, Brittany put a finger to his lips. "I'm so proud of you. Delia told me what you did on Easter. She also said you're planning to pay for Tara's health insurance and help her little girl go to a specialist. But Delia never said you were showing up here."

"I had to convince you in person that we need you on the ranch."

"I was already planning to come back as soon as Dad is out of the hospital."

He hoped he wasn't dreaming. He pulled her back into his arms for another kiss. When the kiss ended, he held her close, his chin resting on the top of her head. "So does this mean you'll marry me?"

"Yes. You are a very special man, and I love you so much."

"Good, because I forgot everything I was going to say when I proposed except one thing. I love you."

Brittany laughed, then kissed him again.

Parker was so happy, it took a minute before he was able to collect his thoughts to speak again.

"You helped me see that I'd only been thinking of myself. I finally realized that if all that bad stuff hadn't happened to me, I would never have met you. And I wouldn't have become a medical writer, which meant I wouldn't know the best doctor for Hailey." Parker nodded. "God can use even the bad things in people's lives to bring about good."

"I'm so glad you realize that now." Brittany smiled as she wiped tears from her cheeks. "Remember when I told you I'd pray for you? See? I knew prayer would work."

Parker grinned. "A June wedding?"

"This June?"

"Yeah." Parker chuckled. "I'm not talking about next June."

"My mom will probably flip out when I tell her we have to plan a wedding in two months."

"We could always elope."

"No way. I want to get married in Pinecrest."

"I think your mom will be happy to arrange that."

Brittany looped an arm through Parker's. "Let's go tell the grandma-to-be our plans."

"Okay, but one more thing." Parker reached into his pocket and pulled out a little velvet box. He opened it. The new ring he'd purchased sparkled. He got down on one knee. "Brittany Gorman, you've made me a better man. Will you marry me?"

Brittany grinned from ear to ear. "Yes and yes and yes. I thought you told me you forgot your speech."

Parker stood and placed the ring on her finger. "I did, but I liked this one better."

"Me, too." Brittany stood on her tiptoes and kissed him again.

* * *

Smiles came from every corner of the little Pinecrest church. Bogey, the ring bearer, sniffed his way down the aisle. Rose and Jasmine followed behind him, leaving a trail of rose and jasmine petals.

Right before Heather, Brittany's maid of honor, joined in the procession, she gave Brittany a hug. "I knew you two would make a great couple."

Brittany's heart swelled with love while she watched Parker taking in the scene. Holding her father's arm, she stepped through the entrance. Parker looked up and smiled. Her heart fluttered like the veil that trailed down her back. Rose and Jasmine's little faces glowed, and Bogey sat as still as a statue while Brittany made her way up the aisle to stand beside Parker.

Surrounded by those they loved, Brittany and Parker repeated their vows to love each other forever. The minister pronounced them husband and wife and told Parker to kiss his bride.

Bogey barked his approval. Laughter filled the air, and joy flooded their hearts. Theirs was a perfect Montana match.

* * * * *

Dear Reader,

Thank you for choosing to read *Montana Match*. When I was a small child my family lived in Montana, so I had fun remembering what it was like to be a little girl, playing in the snow there. I hope you enjoyed this story, which also takes me back to one of my earlier books, *Love Walked In,* set in Pinecrest, Washington, where Brittany lived while she was a teenager.

Forgiveness is a big part of this story and it's a recurring theme in a number of my books. Sometimes it's hard to forgive because the hurt is so deep, but God can give us the strength to forgive. Parker comes to realize the truth of Jesus's words in Matthew 6:14-15: "For if you forgive other people when they sin against you, your heavenly Father will also forgive you. But if you do not forgive others their sins, your Father will not forgive your sins."

I love to hear from readers. I enjoy your letters and emails so much. You can write to me at P.O. Box 16461, Fernandina Beach, Florida 32035, or through my website, www.merrilleewhren.com.

May God bless you,

Merrillee Whren

Questions for Discussion

1. At the beginning of the story, Parker is reluctant to meet Brittany because he is afraid of what she knows about his past. Do you think his concern is legitimate? Why or why not?

2. Brittany has the mistaken idea that Parker is much older than he is. Has there ever been a time when you had a preconceived idea about people until you got to know them better? If so, how did you deal with it?

3. Brittany has recently lost her job. Have you or someone you know lost a job? How did it make you feel? Did it cause you to question God's plan for your life? If so, how did you face this?

4. Rose and Jasmine are identical twins, and Brittany is worried that she might not be able to tell them apart. Have you ever known identical twins? If so, what was your experience in being able to tell them apart?

5. Which scene in the story is your favorite? Explain.

6. Both Brittany and Parker have faced some adverse life situations. Although they both question God, Brittany decides to embrace God as a way to find answers to her problems, while Parker pushes God away. Why do you think these characters chose the path they did?

7. Brittany wonders how she can know what God's will is for her life. Has there ever been a time when you were seeking God's direction? If so, how did you determine

His direction? How do the verses in Proverbs 3:5-6 speak to this question?

8. Brittany wanted a dog when she was a child. Why couldn't she have one? Do you or did you ever have a pet? If so, talk about the importance of the pet in your life.

9. Brittany also had a collection. What was it? Do you collect anything? What is the significance of your collection?

10. Parker can be somewhat of a workaholic. What do you think made him that way? Do you see him changing his attitude toward work during the story? If so, why do you think this happened?

11. What did Parker not look forward to telling Rose and Jasmine? Has there ever been a time when you had to tell someone you love some unsettling news or information from your past? How did you handle it?

12. Parker is touched by his daughters' homemade Valentines. How do you like to celebrate Valentine's Day?

13. When Parker refuses to let Brittany take Rose and Jasmine to see a play in Stockton, Brittany defies him. How do you feel about her actions? Do you think they eventually helped Parker change his mind about letting the girls go into town? Why or why not?

14. Brittany realizes that she can't have a romantic relationship with Parker unless she can accept him as he is. Do

you think this kind of acceptance is important in a relationship? Why or why not?

15. When Parker finally decides to forgive the people who hurt him, he goes to church. His former friend, Larry, reaches out to Parker and helps him make that final move. Has there ever been a time when you had the opportunity to help someone overcome an obstacle in his or her spiritual life? Explain.

INSPIRATIONAL

Wholesome romances that touch the heart and soul.

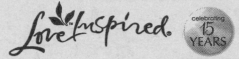

COMING NEXT MONTH
AVAILABLE JANUARY 31, 2012

HOMETOWN HEARTS
The Granger Family Ranch
Jillian Hart

THE LAST BRIDGE HOME
Redemption River
Linda Goodnight

SECOND CHANCE MATCH
Chatam House
Arlene James

ROCKY POINT PROMISE
Barbara McMahon

FALLING FOR THE FIREMAN
Allie Pleiter

A HOUSE FULL OF HOPE
Missy Tippens

REQUEST YOUR FREE BOOKS!

2 FREE INSPIRATIONAL NOVELS
PLUS 2
FREE
MYSTERY GIFTS

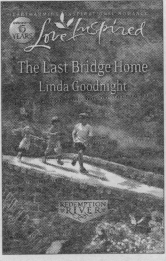

Louisa Morgan loves being around children.
So when she has the opportunity to tutor bedridden Ellie,
she's determined to bring joy back into the motherless
girl's world. Can she also help Ellie's father open his
heart again? Read on for a sneak peek of

THE COWBOY FATHER

by Linda Ford,
available February 2012 from Love Inspired Historical.

Why had Louisa thought she could do this job? A bubble of self-pity whispered she was totally useless, but Louisa ignored it. She wasn't useless. She could help Ellie if the child allowed it.

Emmet walked her out, waiting until they were out of earshot to speak. "I sense you and Ellie are not getting along."

"Ellie has lost her freedom. On top of that, everything is new. Familiar things are gone. Her only defense is to exert what little independence she has left. I believe she will soon tire of it and find there are more enjoyable ways to pass the time."

He looked doubtful. Louisa feared he would tell her not to return. But after several seconds' consideration, he sighed heavily. "You're right about one thing. She's lost everything. She can hardly be blamed for feeling out of sorts."

"She hasn't lost everything, though." Her words were quiet, coming from a place full of certainty that Emmet was more than enough for this child. "She has you."

"She'll always have me. As long as I live." He clenched his fists. "And I fully intend to raise her in such a way that even if something happened to me, she would never feel like I was gone. I'd be in her thoughts and in her actions every day."

Peace filled Louisa. "Exactly what my father did."

Their gazes connected, forged a single thought about fathers and daughters…how each needed the other. How sweet the relationship was.

Louisa tipped her head away first. "I'll see you tomorrow."

Emmet nodded. "Until tomorrow then."

She climbed behind the wheel of their automobile and turned toward home. She admired Emmet's devotion to his child. It reminded her of the love her own father had lavished on Louisa and her sisters. Louisa smiled as fond memories of her father filled her thoughts. Ellie was a fortunate child to know such love.

Louisa understands what both father and daughter are going through. Will her compassion help them heal—and form a new family? Find out in
THE COWBOY FATHER
by Linda Ford, available February 14, 2012.

Love Inspired Books celebrates 15 years of inspirational romance in 2012! February puts the spotlight on Love Inspired Historical, with each book celebrating family and the special place it has in our hearts. Be sure to pick up all four Love Inspired Historical stories, available February 14, wherever books are sold.

Love Inspired®
SUSPENSE
RIVETING INSPIRATIONAL ROMANCE

FITZGERALD BAY

Law-enforcement siblings fight for justice and family.

Follow the men and women of Fitzgerald Bay as they unravel the mystery of their small town and find love in the process, with:

THE LAWMAN'S LEGACY by Shirlee McCoy
January 2012

THE ROOKIE'S ASSIGNMENT by Valerie Hansen
February 2012

THE DETECTIVE'S SECRET DAUGHTER
by Rachelle McCalla
March 2012

THE WIDOW'S PROTECTOR by Stephanie Newton
April 2012

THE BLACK SHEEP'S REDEMPTION by Lynette Eason
May 2012

THE DEPUTY'S DUTY by Terri Reed
June 2012

*Available wherever
books are sold.*

www.LoveInspiredBooks.com